Deep Overstock

#14: Magic
October 2021

META - WICCA/MAGIC

EDITORIAL

EDITORS-IN-CHIEF: Mickey Collins & Robert Eversmann

MANAGING EDITORS: Michael Santiago & Z.B. Wagman

POETRY: Jihye Shin

PROSE: Michael Santiago & Z.B. Wagman

TRANSLATION EDITOR: Vicky Ruan

COPYEDITOR: Leora Joy Jones

COVER: Ōme Tarot Card by Viviann Ruiz

CONTACT: editors@deepoverstock.com
deepoverstock.com

On the Shelves

The Pledge

9 The Kerskiffet Sourhisk Dictionary of Magical Heilungery compiled by Jonathan van Belle

13 The Color of Luck by Jo Griffin

21 A Circle of Witches by Ben Crowley

22 Centos 1-5 by Doris Ferleger

27 A Recipe for Disaster? by Bogdan Groza

29 Grey Hair by Hibah Shabkhez

30 Green Ghost Remembers: The Death of the Wizard by Kate Falvey

31 Wrestling with Magic by Nicholas Yandell

34 Surprising Things by K. B. Thomas

The Turn

43 Awaken by Kummam Al-Maadeed

46 a lesson in technical magic by Timothy Arliss OBrien

48 The Garden of Forking Tongues by Jonathan van Belle

53 Immortalizing: for Yuan Hongqi by Yuan Changming

54 Everything Dies - Magical Antidote #3 by Farnilf P.

56 The Woolgatherers by Kate Falvey

58 The Magic of Living by John Delaney

60 My Grandpa Was a Wizard by Mickey Collins

The Prestige

67 Beyond the Velvet by Michael Santiago

74 Synchrony by Walter Moon

75 Marco Believed in Magic by Lynette Esposito

78 Five Seed Swindle by Ryan Shane Lopez

85 Heroes and Villeins by Desiree Ducharme

90 Magic Act by David James Poissant

94 My Father, the Villain by Eric Thralby

continued...

continued...

97 That shallow, musty grey, almost stagnant creek by Shireen Arora

99 Tiny Babbitt by Rachel Aydt

Letter from the Editors

Dearest Readers,

Magic is the impossible. Whether it's a coin appearing from behind the ear, a rabbit disappearing into a hat, or a double rainbow across the sky, magic is what we wish could happen. It's a suspension of disbelief to just enjoy the moment for what it is. It's hope. And we could all use some hope and magic in our lives now.

This issue, the pieces are divided into the three parts of a magic trick as named by Christopher Priest in The Prestige: The Pledge, The Turn, and The Prestige. Contributors have taken on illusions, magicians, heroes and villeins, life and death, but the constant remains that these pieces promise and deliver on impossibilities that can only be described as magic.

Live in the moments these pieces provide. Return to your childlike wonder. And then turn your attention to the magical bard who was Shakespeare and write those sonnets, scenes, or whatever else, by November 30th.

Best,

Deep Overstock Editors

THE PLEDGE

The first part [of a magic trick] is called "The Pledge". The magician shows you something ordinary: a deck of cards, a bird or a man. He shows you this object. Perhaps he asks you to inspect it to see if it is indeed real, unaltered, normal. But of course... it probably isn't.

Christopher Priest, The Prestige

The Kerskiffet Sourhisk Dictionary of Magical Heilungery

compiled by Jonathan van Belle

(For Maria Franz)

A brief note of introduction is due for this small sample of my larger magical dictionary. There is a perspective, attainable by you, in which, or out of which, reality shines sublimely. But what do I mean, exactly? You've heard it said "Judge not, lest you be judged." I say, simply, "Judge not." Certainly, you will be judged, so what then? Will you now judge, having been judged yourself, perhaps even damned? But what do I mean by this, more precisely? A tale might clarify: There once was an old, bedridden man who lived alone in a small house with a giant crow, some sixteen feet high. This giant crow fed the sickly man like it would feed its own nestlings. Yet, unbeknownst to the man, the giant crow more often than not ate human corpses it had located at various outlying graveyards; this bird had fed the man that regurgitant; the flavor was masked, even made delectable, by the bird's digestive fluids. In summary, if you have the habit of looking at the feet of the homeless, this dictionary is for you. But a warning to you: your teeth may become sea glass and your tongue, your precious tongue, a war-tongue!

Dodklipse: *n.* When persons randomly fade away. Without warning, without reason, they turn semi-transparent, then (in a span of only ten seconds) they grow fully transparent until they totally disappear. There are only ten seconds to realize anything, do anything, say anything. No one knows why it happens, nor why it happens to some and not others. They just fade translucent and vanish. At any moment, anyone may vanish, it is assumed. Some who are missing may be just such cases of vanishment. It is assumed that vanishment means death. A husband wakes to an empty bed. A woman screams to her sister in the next room over, desperate with terror and choked with wishes to stay. It is over in ten seconds.

Eggudru: *n.* Minor deity of gluttony (opposite of deity Igdorbu). Ate his own feces when food was unavailable; developed a taste for it, and now survives off his ever-recycling feces Someone who is "full of shit" or "bullshitting" may be referred to as "Eggudru." When you bullshit, you are said to have "a mouth like Eggudru." Bullshitting itself is called "Eggudru's feast."

Frolly: *n.* A specific ceremonial funeral dance. In a Frolly, the body is hoisted from the tusks of the large elephant-like Gottemdob so that it dangles slightly above the ground (its toes an inch from the dust), and the funeral-goers each have a brief two-partner dance with the body. An animal trainer ensures that the Gottemdob moves so that the body moves gracefully with each funeral dancer.

Gopovogos: A gigantic seashell, like a lace murex shell, used as a communal space in Joya Lahssa, in Koki-pomgo. An aviary of hummingbirds fly inside, feeding those inside a magical nectar; one purses one's lips as if to kiss, and they come, hover near one's lips, and serve one a little serving of the nectar.

Gysskl: A white cacti in southern Urtunoq. For certain species, eating the dry grey flesh of the Gysskl cacti gives the eater a pheromone-like scent that allows the eater to bond with and ride a vungfreysh (see entry on "vungfreysh"), but only while the pheromone-like scent is present; as soon as the scent dips below a certain threshold, the rider is in danger of being killed by the vungfreysh. Frequent vungfreysh riders must eat gysskl as part of every meal, though it tastes "as rancid as a pargantra's blavvort."

Kahlyrot: A nine-bladed urumi sword whose whip-like steel blades have two magical properties: (1) They pass harmlessly through the wielder, i.e., do not slice the wielder; (2) they can only be seen by the wielder, i.e., are invisible to all others.

Kolpahma: Traditional Joya Lahssa "sacred magic" spaces: turf pit-houses with rib-like roof beams of orogilla wood thatched with pink gullip palms and daubed with a baby blue clay. The orogilla's peppery aroma fills the interior.

Kulu: (Native to Koki-pomgo) An orange-colored, banana-shaped fruit with seeds that are neon pink and shaped like crescent moons. Kulu is fruit of the Kulu Vine. Kulu seeds are entheogenic.

Mare Silentii: (Sea of Silence) A sea without wind, high salinity, and only dull gray water.

Snow-swaddled: *slang.* Asleep in somnosurrogacy; "snow" due to the white blindfold.

Somnods (aka Somnosurrogates): Those who "don the ivory" (white blindfolds) and do others' sleeping for them (called "somnosurrogacy").

Uklowen: An apothecary with the ability to shrink people to the size of mosquitos and imprison these helpless people in a chamber inside of his own body (in his thigh near his genitalia).

Voll Godders: Religious self-cannibals. They ingest a chemical (via the glands of an amphibious creature) that stimulates a benign tumescent growth. They harvest their tumescent growths, cook them with other religiously prescribed ingredients, and eat the stuff as a high ritual, called Gom.

Vungfreysh: A tyrannosaurus-like creature in Urtunoq. Two-headed. Covered in white fur. Similar to an electric eel. The vungfreysh is constituted of powerful electrogenic tissues. It spits lightning as a dragon spits fire. Vungfreysh like the taste of yiskiv (see entry on "yiskiv"). One can ride Vungfreysh under two conditions: One must eat gysskl (see entry on "gysskl") and one must wear a "drogdek" (a body suit made of deklornatrag hide) to protect from the vungfreysh's electrical currents.

Vypiofrike: an all-white plant that looks and acts like kudzu vine. Vypiofrike, which Grows in various parts of Qohellonth, is used as wreaths for somnosurrogacy (see entry on "somnods").

Yiskiv: *n.* (Native of Urtunoq) A farmed animal, used for its blue milk, turquoise fur, and fatty meat.

Zuvuq: (Native to northern Nolvisk) A black, lantern-shaped fruit on a shrub with night-blooming black blossoms. Zuvuq is a powerful opioid whose black sap tastes like "the permafrosts of Yoqrin Shoro."

So, lick, lick the zuvuq,
and for god-color, add kulu;
and don the ivory, forever,
for all dodklipse in time,
and all are ghosts from their frolly severed

The Color of Luck
by Jo Griffin

In a perfect world, motherhood would not be equal to loneliness, but hers was not a perfect world.

She was nineteen when she met him, when he took her to the rocky beaches of that town, the town where nothing ever happened and no one ever left, to feed the schools of skyfish together. Holding hands, they'd crumble stale bread and fling it up, towards the clouds, and the schools would swoop at them, a massive fist that pulled back at the last second, and the bread would vanish. He caught one for her once, a tiny goldfish with red fins and white stripes. She admired it through the jar for a while before releasing it back to the winds.

She was twenty-two when he was gone, leaving her alone with two children, a few crumpled bills of pity, and nowhere to go. They say he took a boat to a different island, one where there were cities, and sunshine, and things happened.

For almost a decade she scraped a living from that stagnant town, counting ship sails on the horizon, teaching her children to throw breadcrumbs to the skyfish. The older child, a girl with very dark eyes who never smiled, she named Laki. The younger, a boy with hair like flame, she called Adam. She did not name him for several weeks, for he was born sickly and pale, his life already burning. But he survived.

When Adam was ten and Laki twelve, she's saved enough to leave that stagnant town for a different place. As they sailed away, her children peering over the railings at the seabirds and wincing as the cold spray hit their necks, she tried not to think about the man who'd left on a ship just like this one.

The wind unwound Adam's scarf and it lifted into the air, but she caught it and placed it tenderly back around his neck.

"Don't lose it, Adam." He hardly seemed to notice her, busy pointing out a bright red seabird in the waves below to Laki. The red reminded her of his hair, of the moon Rada. She found it on the horizon at the stern, and offered a silent prayer to the Red Heart of Day. She wasn't sure what she was praying for. Perhaps she just liked to think there was someone watching.

The city they now called home perched on a tiny island at the edge of the world. If you didn't look, you almost wouldn't notice, but eventually you'd realize that the empty expanse behind the city wasn't the sky reflected on the water at all, but the sky itself. They approached the city as the sun was going down, and the void was filled with a red glow, like the last breaths of a fire. The red glow spread to the city, igniting the streets like cracks in a burning log.

Laki asked her if the city was on fire. Their mother assured her that no, it was only lanterns. Every home in the city had one.

"What are the lanterns for?"

"Luck," said their mother.

She'd arranged to rent a small apartment, and though her children begged to see the city, she insisted they wait for morning. The apartment was tiny, perched near the top of a stack of similar cramped homes, a maze of narrow staircases and steep alleys which twisted the shadows. Though they were in the middle of a great city, they felt as though they walked through a dark forest valley.

There was already a lantern above their door. A bit stained and weather worn, but it lit up fine.

That night, she came to check on them as they slept and found Adam's blanket laid neatly back, his ratty pillow missing a head upon it. She found the boy silhouetted against the night, leaning on the railing on the tiny square step outside the front door. He'd turned off the red lantern, and his pajamas billowed in the brisk night wind. A single skyfish darted past, dipping out of the starry abyss for a moment before it vanished in the gloom of the alley below.

"Adam?"

He jumped a bit, then smiled sheepishly.

"What are you doing?"

He turned back to the view of the city below, silent and speckled with their neighbor's red lanterns. There was a sliver of void visible between the buildings.

"Looking," he said quietly.

"Looking at what? It's dark."

"The moons."

She looked up. Laris was almost right above them, full and blue. "There's only one moon at night," she corrected him. "Rada only rises in the day, you know that. And you've seen the moons before, child. Come back inside."

He cast a longing look at Laris and hesitated. "Could… could you tell me the story again?"

"Again?"

"Please?"

She gave a sigh, then dropped a hand onto his head to massage his hair. "Fine, then it's back to bed.

"Rada was not always a moon. He was a boy with red hair who fell in love with Laris. Laris was the only moon then, the Great Blue Eye of Night."

Adam lifted his eyes up to meet the Great Blue Eye and she felt him shiver. "Red hair like me?"

She swallowed. "Yes, red hair like you. He wanted to be with the moon, so he tried to reach it. He flew until his wings gave out, but Laris was no closer, so he fell back to earth and despaired. He tried to lasso the moon, but no matter how much rope he tied together, it was never long enough, and he let the lasso fall with aching arms. Finally, since he couldn't bear to be so far from the moon, he threw himself into the ocean, to swim to where the Great Blue Eye of Night reflected on the waves. His wings grew wet and heavy, and began to drag him down. So he cut them from his shoulders and let them sink beneath the waves, and swam on unburdened.

"But just like one can only fly so high, one can only swim for so long. When the sun rose, he lost sight of the moon and drowned, his arms outstretched towards where Laris had been. The Great Blue Eye of Night saw it happen and wept, and the storm that struck the lands was fiercer than any before it. When the storm clouds faded, and the sun rose again, the people gasped to see a new moon rising with the sun. Rada, the Red Heart of Day, forever separated from his love but rescued by it."

She finished the story. Adam was still staring at Laris, and its reflection filled his eyes. His mother would never admit it, but she'd almost named him Rada, after seeing his bright red hair, desperate that the moon might save her sickly son. It was a good thing she hadn't. The boy already chased the moon enough.

Days became years, and with their mother always work-ing, Laki and Adam often found themselves alone. They were forbidden to wander the city alone, especially to the west where the city hung over the edge of the world, but Laki was old enough now to question everything she was told. So she wan-dered the city and went west, towards the edge of the world. It called to her, that deep void of sky and stars. It told her to wrap her fingers in the mesh wire fence, to put her eye to one of the holes and take in the nothingness below, but she never did. In-stead she'd stand a few feet away and just stare at it, and let the crowds part around her like a rock parts water.

If Laki was a rock, then she was slowly being weathered by the stream. She was quiet and serious, the kind of child adults called "an old soul." The kind of child who grows up too fast. It happened in moments when she thought about the father she'd never met. When she saw how dark the skin around her mother's eyes was getting. When she saw Adam, head tipped back towards the moon he'd never hold. When she watched a man cut through the chain-link fence and give himself to the void. He hadn't even cried. His face had been serene and surrendered, at peace. And Laki imagined herself falling.

All these things she held close to her heart, until the lanterns no longer made her smile, and she drew the curtains at night to block their light.

Once, when Adam was still young, their mother came home and found drawings on a corner of the wall and a guilty Adam hiding in his room. He'd drawn Laki with long black lines, himself as a scribble of red hair, and their mother all in blue. Another mother might've yelled, but the next day when she returned from work, she had a gift for her son. Pencils and crayons and watercolors, and three different paper pads. He'd sit in the kitchen and drag the pencils back and forth until their mother came home, or until it was so dark outside he couldn't see and all he could do was watch the fish swim by, whichever came first.

Sometimes Laki would encourage him to draw on the front porch. It was hardly a porch at all, more a large stair outside the screen door, but he'd fit his knees over the edge and kick open air, sketching the neighbor's red lanterns in the light of their own. Red for good luck. Hang a red lantern by the door and good luck will come to those who cross through it. Sometimes he thought theirs must not be red. Close to red, like vermillion, but not true red. He learned the word vermillion from the wrapper on one of his crayons.

He later realized that Laki encouraged him to sit on the porch because she knew he'd wait there all night for their mother and she could smuggle girls into her room. Boys too, sometimes. Anyone who might also exist in that space of loneliness with her, and perhaps reduce it. She'd help them climb the short distance from the fire escape to the window and his scratching pencils would cover the sounds they made. And so he'd sit in silence, counting each fish that darted past his toes, each rippling school riding the winds far above his head. Sometimes they'd duck down towards their building and cover the sky for a few moments. Sometimes Laki would sit outside too, after her girl had gone, sticking her feet through the railing and letting them dangle beside his. She'd tip stale cereal over the edge and count the seconds as it fell. Sometimes the fish would catch it before it shattered on the concrete. Usually not. The not-quite red lantern made Laki's tears look like blood.

Five years they'd lived in that city at the edge of the world. Their mother came home one night and found Adam, like usual, drawing under the red lantern. Laki had gone out and had not yet returned, so they stayed up together to wait for her. Night fell slowly. Adam watched Rada disappear over the edge of the world, swallowed by the void. Laris wouldn't be out for another few hours.

Laki did not return.

They both began to worry. Adam found himself erasing more than he was drawing, and his mother kept glancing at her watch. She'd been gone a long time, much longer than usual, but she was afraid to speak her worries and make them real.

So instead she just stood up, took her coat, and said, "I'm going to find her."

"I'll stay here," said Adam. "In case she comes back."

His mother nodded and started down the steps, until he called her back. "Wait, take this." And he took down the red lantern. The paper was stained and worn and the candle wavered a bit in the wind, but kept burning.

Wordlessly, she accepted it.

Adam sat back down and realized how dark it was without the lantern for company. When he could no longer see his mother, he bent over his sketchbook and tore page after page free, severing them from the spine. They scattered around him, lifting as the world inhaled, and Adam kept working.

The walk was long and lonely. Her work had her spending long hours on her feet, and by the time she reached the west end of the city, her feet were blistered and her legs ached. She prayed to Laris that she was wrong, but where else would Laki go?

The chain link fence glinted; a thin net stretched across the void. She walked along it, one hand tracing the cold metal, one gripping the red lantern, breathless in the night wind and afraid to peer over the edge. Afraid to see what might lay below. Again she prayed to Laris, the Great Blue Eye of Night, the eye that knows and loves all, to protect her children.

Slowly, Laris rose above the city, big and blue and watching.

She found Laki in a place where the fence had been cut away, the sharp points bent back to make a door-sized hole. She was seated inside, hands folded in her lap, feet dangling over the edge of the world and kicking at the void. She looked up as her mother approached, and her mother's heart twisted at the sight of so many tears.

There was hardly room, but their mother sat beside Laki at the void's edge and put her feet over. She set the lantern in her lap and reached for Laki's hand. She took it, after a moment. They sat like that for a long time, feet swinging in the void, staring at the stars that filled the space beneath the world.

From a cloud far above there came a great sweeping fist, a massive school of fish descending from the heavens. Like the ceaseless future, it flinched at the last second and broke apart to settle gently upon them, a thousand tiny goldfish parting around them like water around rocks in a stream. The mother reached out to gently cup one, it swam over her palm for a long moment before slipping back into the wind. A few of them darted around the lantern, and the candle flickered.

Laki reached for the lantern and her mother lifted it. For a moment, they held it together. A single point of color and light in that endless void.

They released it together. Slowly, gently, the paper was cupped by the wind and carried into the void, where it began to fall. They watched until the red light had vanished completely, just another star.

The world seemed to exhale as they walked home. Lanterns dimmed gently as their candles went out. Families held one another as they slept and dreamed. Laris looked down on the world and saw a mother and her children, alone and yet clinging to one another with the desperation of a candle in the wind, fighting to stay lit. The walk back was a long one, and yet it didn't feel lonely.

They reached their street, the narrow alley filled with staircases and shadows, lit only by their neighbor's red lanterns. The mother had put one foot on the stairs when she heard Laki gasp softly and looked up.

For a moment, she thought she was looking at Laris, but no, the Great Blue Eye of Night was winking far far above them. This light was much closer, a candle shining through a blue paper lantern above their apartment door. She could just make out Adam, paintbrush in hand, going over the paper with paint. When he stepped back, there it was. Their very own Laris, their very own lantern of luck, blue and bright and in fierce denial of the darkness.

A Circle of Witches
by Ben Crowley

When the male witches flew into the river they made a male raft, an enclosed circle of men, and spat from their shoulders, spinning like a wheel.

We chased after them over many bridges, their lips like lilies opening, as they swiftly swept through river towns. I caught the attention of one witch. Our eyes met as we men galloped down stones and they male witches roared up the river. Our lips parted identically--Witch.

Witches are formed from nothing if not from solid air or light, or, at the very least, a haunted coat falling up from the floor. When you are drenched in rain and crying into your wrists, a witch emerges from the trees. He is the one who stands behind you. The witch fills up with magic as the ground fills up with men.

We lost them in the mouth of a bridge. We had run until our shoes were scraps and we knew no language, all because we had now seen magic. The witch at the bar had appeared a rosebud from his sleeve. We had seen him snap his fingers, and we had seen the rosebud bloom before us. We needed more.

Centos 1-5
by Doris Ferleger

CENTO 1: MY ECHOING COUNTRY
(*Marrying Neruda's* Love Poems *with Rukeyser's* Book of the
Dead *mining disaster poems*)

In love you have loosened yourself like seawater.
Or uneasy, wounded by me.

In my body, bells,
dove wings with eyes tired

of my echoing country
and its thrust of live coals, of fluttering flag.

Hide me in your arms
with the living and the dead

walking tranquil in fire-dreams filled
with velocities and misfortunes.

Lodge me at your back, oh shelter me.
Everything carries me to you,

to our house
of the heart where I have roots

upon the earth and upon
the winds and upon the waters.

CENTO 2: RIVER OF ROUND HARDNESS
(*Lines from Neruda's* Love Poems *and Rukeyser's* Book of the
Dead *poems*)

When you go into me, crystalline,
this is the most audacious landscape:

your skin, a bell filled with grapes,
crosscut by snow, wind at the hill's shoulder.

The hill makes breathing slow, slow breathing after
you row the river of round hardness.

We shall always be, you and me,
sealed by fire.

And we shall always be strangers.

CENTO 3: DEUS EX MACHINA
(*Lines from Neruda's* Love Poems *and Muriel Rukeyser's* Book of
the Dead)

If each day
or is it only now—

because there is a dark room and a broken candleholder
and its warlike form, its dry circle—

a flower appeared like a drop—
flower of sweet total light—

how triumphal and boundless
the orbit of white—
~
if each day
or is it only now

I surrendered to the broken candle-
holder of light

surrendered to the flower
disappearing like a drop

of night—how triumphal
and boundless this orbit of sight—

SEMI-CENTO 4: TO VANISH AND RETURN
(*Lines altered from Lynda Hull's* Collected Poems)

Night sky, sapphire. Crescent
brooch of white. Moonlight

cracks against asphalt.
Thick gray hair wraps her shoulders.

To vanish and return
transformed does not take

dying. Takes the pain of staying
the same one day more,

takes peonies exploding.
Why must it take so long

to value the fog and the quick dark?

CENTO 5: EXTINGUISHED OR FORGOTTEN
(*Lines from Muriel Rukeyser's* Book of the Dead)

In me nothing is extinguished or forgotten.
At night I get up to catch my breath.

Yes. There is difficulty breathing.
I am trying to say it as best I can.

The commerce of silences and mysteries.

A Recipe for Disaster?

by Bogdan Groza

Let us start with the fundamentals, the first thing that you will need is an alchemic circle, for there the essence of Truth converges and through it everything flows. Bear in mind that not just any circle will suffice, you will have confine within it a square, each point of its angles touching the circumference. These lines shall be traced with the ash that will be willingly provided by a phoenix upon its molting.

Within this circle, you shall place a vessel made out of the intertwined viridian leaves from the tree of Eons. Hence, you shall add a liquid basis: it must be the purest of morning dews that may be recovered only from within the frail buds of snowdrops.

Now it is time to add the other quintessential ingredients. First and foremost a pinch of infinity, but no more than that for even a speck more would lead to dire consequences. Then mix in two grains of sand from the hourglass of Eternity; this is important, one grain shall be taken from the top, from the time that is yet to come, and one from the bottom, from the sand that has already completed its journey. I am sure that Eternity, in its vast magnanimity, will not mind sharing. Start to stir gently in a helical pattern by using a perfectly smooth and straight branch from the World Tree. You will need to carefully put in a dash of the silence found at the Abyssal Firmament and a touch of noise from the first Great Explosion—as that from the second one just won't do. Continue to mix the elixir as you do not want it to run rampant, trust me on this. The glimmer obtained through a kaleidoscope of diamonds will give the compound the spark that we need. We are slowly getting there.

Now add an apple.

Once all this is done, you shall place four flakes of incandescent magma taken from the very core of the world, one on each corner of the square that you have previously traced. These specks of molten rock that would otherwise have only destructive properties will make the contents of the vessel boil and a gentle vapor will start to form. Now you will need to transmogrify said vapor, else it would become a malicious miasma, and that would be vexing indeed. To do so you shall cool it with the breeze that flows beyond the limits of the zenith, the one that caresses the cerulean stars and alabaster constellations.

If you have followed these instructions correctly, then the condensed vapor will finally take the form of a delicate creature; the components that were used will be imbued in it. I am very fond of this creation and think I shall call it a human being.

I, one of the Ten Sages of Lore, kindred to Eternity and bound to Truth end here my notes. I fear I must however forewarn my dearest colleagues: if even one step of this procedure is forlorn, if any component eschewed or not of the purity required, the end result could be catastrophic. This creature, this human, has the ability to surpass our expectations and even ourselves, but only if made as I engraved here. I am unwavering in thinking that tampering with this formula would only lead to a situation we would be unable to face.

Grey Hair
by Hibah Shabkhez

Each grey hair I grow has powers unknown
To all but the torchlight that never blinked
In the storm that unlit our beacons, thrown
Into darkness by the ardour that winked

And sputtered hope. All the while that serene,
Stolid tube of trapped and vapid light stared
On, through the thunder, at the drowning green
Faces and porches standing almost bared

Of their ramparts of privilege. But dare
We raise cold grace to the rank of the hiss
Of log-fires, of candles' need to care
For us? Do we forget to treasure this?

Better to feign and mourn a Love unfelt
And sneak, secretless, into a sphinx's pelt

Green Ghost Remembers: The Death of the Wizard

by Kate Falvey

I skulk around the gemmy corners of the emerald
mausoleum and sift the twinkling dirt through the veil
of my unnatural hand, as if memories of sentience
were enough for me to hold the insubstantial
grandeur of our lofty and unseemly dreaming.

Never was I bold enough to challenge his dominion.
All the brilliant green has gone with his demise, leaving
smears of gaseous sheen on stony faces and stone-faced
pediments, on avenues and temperaments,
on makeshift palaces, and shifty, feckless eyes.

When he plummeted to earth the second time, his luck
cracked into a trillion feeble facets. The glare
of his bedeviled, shattered might flared through our
conundrum of a world leaving a muddy mangled corpse
and the aching dust of our belief in reanimating magic.

We buried him with pomp and spectacle, befitting all his
vainglory and our unavailing need for ritual enchantment.
Then the light became translucent and then bleary,
like a cheap and transient midway or an after-hours arcade
as if the bill for our electricity was never fully paid.

And so I haunt, with glazy green confusion, the minds of Oz's
children. I was a palace maid before the palace sputtered out.
My dust mop glitters and my apron strings trail sparks.
Even then I knew the bargain for this temporary emerald
was struck between his vision and the unremitting dark.

Wrestling with Magic
by Nicholas Yandell

1. An Inquiry

Is magic
The physical manifestation of imagination?

The power to plunge into fantasies
And never have to leave?

Make life more like dreams
Or bouts of creativity?

Freeing the luster of stories
From material possibilities?

Taking reality
In whatever direction
We might see it go.

Is it something we see?
Something we do?
Something we feel?

Some mystical force
Interacting concretely
Molding impossible unknowns
Into the tangible and relevant?

Do we really have to know
What magic is
To bask in its benefits?

Or is it best experienced
By those who acknowledge
That the power of magic
May lie in its mystery?

2. An Encounter

When I've encountered magic
It's never some display
Of sparks
Or smoke
Or dust
Or flame.

It's just a stretching
Of my understanding
Of what reality
Actually is.

It doesn't have to be
A drastic departure.

Just a hair outside
The realm of possibility.

A happening
That can't be
Explained away
Successfully.

Leaving one exposed
To the mist
Of the irrational
Watering
The spinning seeds
Taking root
In the cracks
Of an existential foundation.

3. A Journey into the Void

I'm unwilling to fully embrace reality.

I won't acknowledge
Solely what my senses register.

From outside possibilities
In art and creativity
And dreams
Dragging me
To places I've never known
Through open doors
To rooms
Denying rationality
And restoring
The wonders of belief.

I can't embrace
A limited view
Any longer.

Abandoning unknowns
Just isn't feasible
When my ambition
Is so much more defined
Than any explanation of actuality.

If there's magic in the void
I want to find it.

So go ahead
Just leave me:

Clinging to fantasies

Living enchanted possibilities

And straddling the edge of imagination

I'm happiest here.

Surprising Things
by K. B. Thomas

It was spring when Mrs Pohvalich went down to her husband's workshop in the basement and hammered together a sign declaring: Palms Read.

"Yelena," said her husband, Morris, as he watched her struggle up the steps, plywood board in tow, "where are you going with that?"

"To the front yard. Open the door for me, please," she said, and he obediently held the door open and watched as she planted the sign in the half-thawed ground. It tilted lazily to one side but Mrs Pohvalich seemed satisfied.

"Morris, where are our lawn chairs?"

"What lawn chairs?" asked Mr Pohvalich, who had last seen the chairs in question some fifteen years before, when their boys had been small and liked to run through the sprinkler in shorts. Before puberty, before sports and cars and girls.

Mrs Pohvalich shook her head and brushed by him, hammer dangling lightly from her fingers.

"We never had any lawn chairs," said her son, Tony, who was busily lifting barbells in a corner of the living room.

"What do you know about it?" asked Mr Pohvalich. "Put down those weights and go take your mother's sign out of the yard. Palms read! What does Yelena Pohvalich know about reading anyone's palms?" he shouted.

Mrs Pohvalich came up from the basement with two lawn chairs in her grip. "I want something done in this house, I do it myself." She unfolded the chairs' aluminum frames, dusted at them with a dish towel, and waited for her first customer.

================================

"My grandmother learned from her grandmother," Yelena Pohvalich told the woman who sat uncomfortably in the lawn chair next to her own. "There's no telling how far back this tradition goes."

Doris Kuchek listened intently, strips of plastic weave suffering under her weight. She'd seen through the slats of her blinds the brawny figure of Tony Pohvalich pulling what looked like a sign from in front of the house and watched as Mrs Pohvalich patiently hammered the sign back into place.

They're moving, thought Mrs Kuchek, and she slipped a scarf over her hair and walked across the street to see for herself.

"This is a tradition?" asked Mrs Kuchek. "Putting lawn chairs in front of the house and offering to tell the future?"

"One great-grandmother sold love potions to young women in Bulgaria. The potions were made of frog parts and the crushed bodies of spiders," Mrs Pohvalich said matter-of-factly.

"I only came over because I thought you were moving," Mrs Kuchek said. "I saw the sign in the yard."

"My own grandmother taught me some of what she knew," continued Mrs Pohvalich. "Give me your hands, Doris. I'll read them."

Mrs Kuchek held her hands tightly in her lap. "I just wanted to know why you were moving."

Gently, Mrs Pohvalich took Mrs Kuchek's hands and held them in her own.

"Do not resist, Doris. Do not be afraid."

"But what if I don't want to know the future?"

"Not even a little bit?" asked Mrs Pohvalich, smiling.

"Well, maybe a little. But what if it's something horrible?"

Mrs Pohvalich closed her eyes and spoke in a strong voice. "At six o'clock my son Tony will take a shower and use up all the hot water. My other son Andrei and his wife Katya are coming for dinner with us. Andrei will eat all the rolls and Katya will refuse everything except a piece of lettuce and three glasses of wine. She'll offer to help with the dishes but I'll be afraid to let her handle the glassware. Besides, there won't be any hot water. Morris will fall asleep in his chair watching the ten o'clock news. That's my future, Doris. How could yours be any worse?"

Challenged, Doris Kuchek gave in. "Do you charge for this?"

"This isn't as difficult as a love potion," Mrs Pohvalich explained, unfolding Mrs Kuchek's hands and tracing the creases with a fingertip. "There are no smelly toadstools to boil or blood to mix with bone. For you, Doris, the first one is free."

=============================

That night at the dinner table Mr Pohvalich advised his family. "Whatever you do, don't encourage her." His wife was in the kitchen. "I don't think it's serious, yet, and maybe if we don't talk about it she'll forget. Women sometimes go a little nuts when they get older." He couldn't bring himself to say the word *menopause*, not in front of his daughter-in-law.

"Not serious!" exclaimed Andrei, piling his plate high with rolls. "My mother starts behaving like a gypsy and you don't think it's serious?"

"I am not behaving like a gypsy," yelled Mrs Pohvalich from the kitchen. "Gypsies ride in wagons and have gold teeth."

"She sure impressed Mrs Kuchek," Tony informed them.

"Mrs Kuchek! Now she's done it! There'll be a line of women out there tomorrow, waiting to have their fortunes told!" Andrei prophesied.

"We could make a fortune from this," Tony divined.

Mr Pohvalich, stricken by the tragedy that had befallen his

family, did not speak again that evening. After dinner he retired to his chair in front of the tv where he was destined to fall fast asleep. He dreamed of expensive gynecologists, of Jungian analysts, of naturopaths in white lab coats, all of whom told him that for what ailed Yelena Pohvalich, they could find no cure.

==============================

Katya visited the next day.

"Mother Pohvalich," she implored, "won't you please tell my fortune?"

"My grandmothers used to sell love potions to the young girls in Romania," began Mrs Pohvalich, "but they never sold one to their own families."

"They weren't up to robbing their relatives, is that it?" shouted Mr Pohvalich from the other room. "Or poisoning them with crushed frogs?"

His wife ignored him. "Some people are foolish and let love take them where it will," she said to Katya. "Some are foolish and never let love take them anywhere at all."

"Do any men ask to have their palms read?"

"Don't encourage her!" instructed Mr Pohvalich from the depths of his chair. "She'll forget all about this!"

"Oh, men," said Mrs Pohavlich with a decisive wave of a hand. "They'd rather not know the future. They don't have the *rezistenţă*, the strength."

"Now you speak Romanian?" yelled Mr Pohvalich. "Men make the future! We don't need you to tell us what's going to happen."

Sighing, Yelena Pohvalich took Katya's right hand into her own. "Daughters, my darling. You are going to have six lovely daughters, and they will be the light of your long life."

"Oh! Mother Pohvalich! Is that what you foresee?" asked

Katya.

"No, my sweet. It is what I hope for."

===============================

"This is the last fortune I shall tell," said Mrs Pohvalich a week later. Doris Kuchek sat with her at the dining room table.

"The last? Why, Yelena, when there is so much more waiting to be told?"

"Coffee, Doris?" Mrs Pohvalich poured from the percolator. "Cream?"

"When did you decide this?" asked Mrs Kuchek, determined. Nothing so exciting as a fortune teller on her own block had happened before and such occurrences are not let go of easily.

"My grandmothers knew when it was time to stop. Wars, famines, plague could not keep them from practicing their art. But when the time comes, there's no getting around it."

"I noticed the sign was missing from the front yard," confessed Mrs Kuchek. "That's why I came over."

"Give me your hands, Doris."

Yelena Pohvalich peered deeply into the lines decorating Doris Kuchek's palms. "I am not an entertainer, here to amuse," she said. "I could tell you things you don't want to hear. Things you don't want to know about and will hate when they happen."

Mrs Kuchek squirmed in her seat. "I distinctly remember that I left the oven on at home. And the iron."

"You came to hear pretty stories about handsome men and new cars. Air conditioning and all wheel drive."

"What do I care for a new car?" asked Mrs Kuchek, aghast, because a new car was her dream. Red exterior paint and leather seats.

"You just want to hear about your husband's future accident and how much you'll get from the insurance ruling," continued Mrs Pohvalich. "You want to know when the airlines are going to reduce their rates and what number you should choose in the lottery."

"You could tell me what number?"

Mrs Pohvalich tossed her head like a coquette. "Of course I could. It's no easy trick, mind you. My own mother told me how. She used to whisper such things when I was little."

"Would you tell me?" breathed Mrs Kuchek, hardly daring to ask. "Just one tiny number?"

"You won't be satisfied with one number and week after week you'll be on my doorstep, asking for more, for bigger and better numbers."

"I won't. I promise," pledged Mrs Kuchek.

And so Yelena Pohvalich, in whose veins flowed the blood of women who once sold love potions to the young girls of Bulgaria and perhaps even Croatia and Kosovo, whispered in the waiting ear a number that, if used correctly, would yield surprising things.

THE TURN

The second act is called "The Turn". The magician takes the ordinary something and makes it do something extraordinary. Now you're looking for the secret... but you won't find it, because of course you're not really looking. You don't really want to know. You want to be fooled. But you wouldn't clap yet.

Christopher Priest, The Prestige

Awaken
by Kummam Al-Maadeed

He finds her sitting on top of the kitchen's table, a hand holding a book, *Dark Side of the Universe*, and her other one lifts an apple to her mouth. She bites and chews. Peeking through her dark long hair, her eyes, those ruby eyes he missed, focused on the book.

How is this possible? She isn't supposed to wake up for another 260 years. This didn't make sense. Who woke her and, more importantly, which side did she choose this time? Is she here to bring peace or create chaos?

He doesn't know what to do, how to deal with this. He's used to a life without her, without them. He's unprepared. The image of his wife and little boy sleeping soundly upstairs brings him terror. Is she here to hurt them? Does she even know they exist?

And as if she read his mind, she looks up at him, the book sliding from her hand and she says, "I see you've started a family."

His fists relax at the gentleness of her words. She is choosing peace. He hoped.

"Isn't it wrong to have a family?" she says; the corner of her lips rise and her eyes gleam. Her soft features twist into a feline glare, killing the hope and lighting a fire in his heart. The spark reminded him of his powers. The powers that could destroy cities at the snap of his fingers. The power he hid for almost a century.

Dropping the apple, she crosses her legs. She looks so thin, like a starving model. Oh, how he forgot how fragile they were after they awaken. She wore a long leather coat that hugged her slim form and brown pants that hid under an ankle boot. She's already familiar with the fashion of this decade. This means she's been here a while. Unlike him, she had time to prepare.

The last time he woke up, he felt lost, empty and simply bored. He didn't want to play the game anymore and with that came the decision of stopping the pattern he loved and hated so much.

"You don't understand our language anymore?" she hisses, tilting her head.

"I understand," he replies, his voice steady. He will never show weakness. He is and will always be the strongest of them all. "And having a family is not wrong."

She climbs down from the table and glides toward him like poisonous mercury dancing on a mirror.

"It's just so…"—she circles him, one hand sliding from his chest to his back—"unfair." She stops before him.

"When did chaos care about fairness?" *How is she awake?*

She tsks. "Oh, but that's what we do, dear peace. We bring balance to the world. We're not meant to live it. Or,"—she grabs his shirt and pulls him closer, hissing—"was that a lie you told me before you cracked the skull of the one I loved two slumbers ago." Her eyes flare with anger.

He remembers that day like it was yesterday. It was one of the rare times they chose to be on opposite sides. It was his idea to be chaos while she was at peace. She never truly forgave him for that fight. He should've known.

"It's part of the game, you said," she spits, her fingers digging into his chest. "We control life, right?"

Before he releases his power at her, she lets go and snaps a finger.

Every frame that holds a photo of his family cracks.

"You think I will allow you to harm them?" He is fed up

with her games. "I don't care how you woke up. Let's not forget who is more powerful and if I put you under once, I will do it again."

He lets his power seep through his eyes and fingers, intimidating her. But she only … laughs.

"Oh, darlin.'" She tries to calm her laughing fit, her hands on her stomach, "You're so cute. Oh darlin.' You thought you could escape the game."

She straightens. Her features sharp, eyes gleaming red, her powers rippling around them.

She stands before him, darkness incarnate.

"All of us are awake darlin' and we are all coming for you."

a lesson in technical magic
by Timothy Arliss OBrien

Written with an artificial intelligence word list generator.

1. the magic of technology

long ago
the solemn presence
warned night

purplish black crystal traveling
what remembered his name

not even hope
was there

the winged edge falls
out the globe

many centuries since
magic still lingered

but technology prevailed

steel can always adapt
lateral balance is what invisible magic was

pagan hands work quite extraordinarily

the results the most disdainful

enchanting light yells coldly
absolute beauty make them aware

the sky and the earth dare me

the touched one rings

you smile

2. the technology of magic

breathing silver

you awaken

there is indescribable

you rebellious wolf

the intermission must understand you
say certainly

retain that ecstasy
left like hope
the fall belongs

the tombstone the globe fantastic
supernatural
lovers into shroud
does not exist

intolerable
noises

more

tonight humanity can finish

glance
don't receive

you are longer
willing
recognize human
this claim

and conclude

the work not done

The Garden of Forking Tongues

by Jonathan van Belle

"Consider what is required," said Gregor, "for something to be deemed a fact. There must first be a world, in some sense of world, to ground this thing called *fact*. How could the fact 'water freezes' be a fact without the existence of water? How could the fact 'there are tortures wherever there are men' be a fact without tortures?"

"Do all facts require a world or ground? 1 is a number. 1 plus 1 equals 2. Those facts don't seem dependent on the existence of any world." Justine lifted her flute of champagne to her lips, and paused, and let the champagne shore up a little around the flute's cusp. "What's a world? We're speaking so liberally of 'world', or, in your hedging phrase, 'some sense of world'; we're presuming worlds now."

"We're being tentative," Don said, leaning against a wall in the corner of the room, lightly and absent-mindedly brushing a bouquet of sweet violets with his forefinger.

"No, it's a fair move," said Gregor, "fair and—well, fair. And I don't have a ready-made reply. My first temptation involved a circular definition: The world is just the totality of facts."

"My guess will still suffer from circularity, but might we allow for a plurality of worlds by this definition: A world is any set of facts." Don tilted his head downward, feeling doubt and thinking of objections to his suggestion. "I'm willing to bite the bullet and accept the counterintuitive consequences of my definition: that a non-empty set is a world; that the set of all facts about shoelaces constitutes a world; and so on."

"Does this allow for worlds that are literally made out of the abstracta of sets? If so, there may be a world that's just the set of all sets that are not members of themselves. It would be a bizarre, contradictory world."

"Let's christen such degenerate worlds with the name: Justine Worlds."

"No thanks, Gregor; I'm a simple prophet—not a Creator."

"It's distasteful, yes," Don interrupted, "but does our distaste mean anything or do any work?"

Justine sipped her sparkling drink, then sipped again. "No, it doesn't." A third sip. "Is this champagne a world?"

"It might be, given the price I paid for it." Gregor enjoyed his joke more than the others. Then a flash of lucidity overwhelmed him; he became, suddenly, sullen. "There's something wrong here."

"Something wrong with my definition?" Don asked.

"No."

"I fail to believe that," Don said. "There must be some error in my nonsense."

"I'm not talking about that," stressed Gregor.

"What are you talking about, then?"

"Don, give him a moment," Justine said, noticing the almost lightless eyes on Gregor's face.

"Are you feeling well, Gregor?"

"Gregor," Justine said, setting down her glass, "do you need something? What is it that's wrong?"

"Our world. This."

Justine and Don waited, one patiently and the other impatiently, for more. Gregor looked both of them directly in the eyes, moving his gaze back and forth between them.

"I know that I see your eyes, but that's it. Something's

wrong with that."

"What do you mean?"

"What do you mean, Don? Look at my eyes. Do you see them?"

Don looked at Gregor's eyes. "Yes, I see them."

"What else do you see?—and observe yourself as carefully as you possibly can."

Don looked around for a moment. "I see many things."

"What do you see specifically? Stop being imprecise."

Don focused his gaze on Justine's flute of champagne. "I see Justine's flute of champagne."

"Now close your eyes and try to reconstruct our location. Call to your mind the details of our location: the furniture, the textile patterns of the furniture, the time of day, any sounds in the background. You too, Justine. The both of you."

"Alright," said Justine, closing her eyes.

"What occurs to you first?" Gregor's voice floated through Justine's awareness like a breeze through a mist.

"A bouquet of violets," Justine said.

"Me too—violets," Don added. "And the champagne glass."

"Anything else? Justine, you? Anything else?"

"I know where *we* are," Justine said, her inflection of "we" suggested that Justine was entertaining a lightly mocking thought.

"No, that's untrue, Justine. You don't. None of us do. It is certain to us that we know, but we don't know. Somehow we're under some magic spell of false judgments. Describe my face, Justine."

"Your face? It's, well—your eyes are—." Justine opened her eyes and looked anxiously at Gregor.

"Now you see. There's no fact about my face. There's no face. You somehow know that you're looking at me, but there's nothing you're looking at. You know that you're looking at me, at Gregor, but that's all you can determine—that's all that's true in your experience."

Don opened up his eyes and also searched for Gregor's face. "Gregor, stop. I know I'm looking at you. I'm looking at you right now."

"Yes, but describe what you see."

"It's you. It looks like you."

"Yes, but what do I look like?"

Don felt like looking away, looking back to the violets, ignoring the confusion. "You look like—you're a man. You look like a man."

"I have a name that's more commonly given to males; that's all that you're saying now. You're inferring my appearance. You see it too, you and Justine. Stop pretending! Be lucid!"

"I don't understand your point," Justine said, picking up and drinking her champagne nervously. "I know I'm looking at you, yet you claim I'm not."

"Incorrect. Wrong. False! You believe you're looking at me, but that's it, that's the whole of it—there's nothing else. There's no object you're looking at, Justine. It's dreamlike; in dreams, you might find yourself absolutely certain that you're a zebra flying through the sky, and yet there's no visual information, no aroma, no audio, no texture. Nothing. Just the delusion. It's like that in this case. You're insurmountably convinced that there's a world of rich detail and decoration around us, and that there's an 'us' with pastness and extension and agency. There's nothing like that."

"Why?" asked Don.

"How am I going to answer that? 'Why?' to you, Don. Why is it, Don? You haven't realized the problem, if that's all you have to say."

"Are we in one of my Justine Worlds?" Justine smirked, but then she felt a vast weightlessness come over her; she realized she couldn't picture her own smirk. Nor her face. Nor her body. "Gregor?"

"Justine?" Gregor could not see Justine. "Shout to me, Justine."

"Gregor? Can you hear me? Don? Don't play with me!"

"Justine?" Don called out, desperate with fear. "Gregor?"

"Don? Justine?" whispered a trembling voice. "Please, answer."

"Gregor? Don?"

"Help me!" cried some depersonalized voice.

Immortalizing: for Yuan Hongqi

by Yuan Changming

Buried deep in the topsoil
Of his native village, my father's ash
Was swirled up in a tornado, joining
All the gods in Taoist legends high
Up in the western sky. He certainly
Has no idea if he can become a Buddha
As he wished; nor did he know he would
Leave earth in such magic manner, but as I
Look up afar into the heart of the universe, I see
A new star sparkling like his bone chip
Glittering in the urn, which I opened to see
Out of curiosity on my way to Shisanbao.
Where are you in this moment, dear Dad?
Still down in the land or up there in the sky?

Everything Dies
Magical Antidote #3
by Farnilf P.

Everything dies.
From the ant you
just stepped on
to the chickens
being slaughtered
down the road.
Everything dies.

Everything dies.
They say you'll
go on, live after.
They have no proof.
It's probably lies.
Desperate wanting.
Everything dies.

Everything dies.
From your favorite
TV show to your
secret dream.
One day they'll
send copies of our
neurons to the cloud.
But we'll still be dead.
Everything dies.

Everything dies.
Cities and forests,
mountains and planets.
The earth will die,
as the sun, the universe
and the multiverse.
Everything dies.

Everything dies.

From your cat and
dog to your grandpa
and grandma.
Graveyards fill up and
crematoria smolder.
Everything dies.

Everything dies.
From your mom
and dad, to you.
You will die.
Everything dies,
you too.
Everything dies.

Everything dies.
Life eats life,
and death, as ever,
serves the drinks.
To die, you have to live.
You are alive, for now.
But time dies too.
Everything dies.

Everything dies.
The symbols we scratch,
the people we love,
the things we hate.
It all goes still,
unwound, silent.
The rot and riot of life.
Everything dies.

The Woolgatherers

by Kate Falvey

Millie and Adela waggle their tow-sacks
through the stile, grazing the beech hedge
as if they were moony golden sheep instead of

moony dun girls meant to be sharp-eyed,
not dozy and slack, watching for bits of fluff,
flimsy in the scraggly brush.

They trod on silver thistle, quaking grass,
bramble, and brome, plucking buttercups
and bluebells instead of Cotswold wool tufts

as they ramble toward the wych elm with
its withered arms scratching at the lowering sky
and giddy at their coming.

Jasper, George, and little Letty Hawkins
scramble close behind, pockets and
willow baskets trembling with unease

and wispy snags of fleece picked from
splintered slat and seedpod,
roughened creeping vine.

There is no spell that will make the boys
quicken to their tasks or give Letty longer,
bolder legs or make the fiddle-riffs of lapwings

less eerily enticing or the yellow whisperings
of lady's bedstraw less lulling, less
beguiling in the webs of shivery light.

Millie and Adela drop their sacks and drag
the boys along within the dreadful rushing
of their voiceless howling, their feet still

sniffing the spongy ground
for little Letty as they dash through

her sudden vanishing.

Through the blue and yellow flower froth,
they whirl their arms and pell-mell hare away,
past the tell-tale milk-blue twitch of thread

whimpering from the lowest grasping
wych elm branch where
little Letty's basket fell

and nowadays is a small tussock
fluffed with yarrow and
wreathed by wild windflowers.

The Magic of Living
by John Delaney

Out of the proverbial top hat,
like a rabbit, pulled.
Imagine that
was your beginning!

The tooth fairy,
Santa Claus,
imaginary
friends with extraordinary
powers turned your focus
into addiction
with hocus-pocus
and fiction.

Language lent
a sleight-of-hand
to every word
that you would understand.
It could animate the heartless,
motivate the remote,
dictate the absurd—
then capture
the impossible, conjure up
the invisible.

With youth and health
you could pretend
there was no end.

Love made you a mind reader;
compassion and forgiveness,
a sword-swallower.

Everything was billed
as "death-defying"
because you were a survivor.
The days spilled
over.

Even in hard times
your soft smile
could fool us,
and make-believe
this was worth your while.

All acts would lead
to your straitjacket escape,
when the drums rolled
as they drew back
the black drape
and opened the locks:

a shroud of linen in an empty box.

My Grandpa Was a Wizard

by Mickey Collins

My grandpa was a wizard. He may not have looked it; he didn't have a beard or wear a cape, but he was magical. Most people may think that their own grandpa is a magician of sorts, just because they're able to pull nickels from behind an ear or he has the power to put you to sleep with their stories. But not my grandpa.

He didn't come from a family of magic. His dad, uncles, and aunt all were in the military. His own grandpa was a principal and later a mayor. Those were probably the least magical careers if ever there was one.

They certainly didn't teach him magic, but they did teach him the worth of hard work and that if you put your mind to something you can accomplish it. So when he wanted something his mind was made up, he was going to do it. He had a fake-it-til-you-make-it attitude, which was helpful in his line of work; making someone believe in you even if that thing isn't there is a wizard's bread and butter afterall. He had confidence and drive.

The first trick he taught me was how to balance a spoon on my nose. He would get the entire table trying doing it. Then while the spoon was successfully in front of your mouth or while you were scrambling on the ground to find your dropped spoon, he'd sneak a bite of your dessert. "Grandpa!" He'd take the cherry off of your sundae, or ask for one of the stems from your Shirley Temple, then pop it in his mouth, only to pull it out again tied in a knot.

The trick he was best known for was his smile that brightened the room, bringing laughter and joy to all around him. You could never be in a bad mood in his presence. He was always prepared to help others, even at the expense of his time or money. He knew something that no one else did: you could be the richest, most powerful wizard, but that didn't matter if you didn't treat others with basic respect and decency.

He was a world traveler. He'd seen and done awe-striking things, but he always said his greatest gift wasn't any of his magical talents or earthly possessions, but the family he had. He was prouder of his family and what they accomplished than anything he ever did. Despite his ability to pull rabbits from hats, he was amazed when you told him you got a B on your report card.

He loved what he did. He worked hard enough that he was able to pick what he wanted to focus on.

So it came to our surprise when he announced that he would be putting on one final show. Wizards live infamously long lives and have long storied careers.

He began the show with an empty stage. Dry ice smoke filled the floor. And then poof! From nothing he suddenly appeared.

The first trick he did was climbing a free-standing ladder. Once he reached the top he pulled a second one from the one he was standing on and he climbed that as well, and then he continued to climb up and up as if he were using rungs that weren't even there. Because he believed he could, even when other people said he couldn't or if he didn't know how. He was a risk-taker.

The audience applauded and oohed and aahed as he climbed back down to the ground. He took a quick bow. He wasn't too proud to take acclaim for his accomplishments.

Once the assistants had removed the ladders off stage, he returned to the center stage. He made a show of pulling up his jacket's sleeves. And then he snapped his fingers and in each of his hands appeared a single penny. He cupped his hands together and the two pennies became one larger penny.

Another round of applause.

He's planned one final trick for us, he says. He spoke softly yet no one had trouble hearing him. He plans to disappear. It wouldn't be the first time. He'd pulled off various disappearing acts, when he would step behind a door only to appear in another, or transport himself from one box on the left side of the stage to the right side and back again. But he promises us this time is different.

A large closet was wheeled onstage behind him. It was ornate, hand carved dark wood. It was built by him, he'd always been a hands-on guy. He removed his suit jacket. And then he took his time unbuttoning his shirt, explaining the trick as he went down. And then there he stood. He was skinnier than I remembered; he joked that his doctor had always advised him to lose a few pounds to lighten the mood.

The assistants spun the closet around, proving there was no funny business. No fishing wire, no trapdoors, no mirrors. This was to be all him. A culmination of his hard work.

He opened the closet door with some effort. Before he closed the door behind him, he took a final look at everyone around him. And smiled. And then the door closed. We heard it lock. And then a silence fell over us.

It was some time, we didn't know when the door would reopen. There wasn't the traditional second closet for him to reappear in this time. We looked around the theatre. Where would he appear from? Surely, any minute now there he would be, in his shirt and jacket again, all of us choosing to ignore that those items were right on the stage where he'd left them. He would pop up behind us, and then ask us to dinner, his treat.

Eventually, one of the assistants went to the closet and ventured to open it up. They hadn't practiced this particular trick, no one knew what was supposed to come next.

Inside the closet, it was true he had disappeared. There was no one in the closet. All there was was a book resting on the bottom of the closet.

He had left behind his magic book that contained all of

his spells. These were his secrets for his life of wizardry. Opening it up revealed just three sentences. They weren't in Latin, they didn't cause rabbits to be pulled from hats, or women to be sawed in half. They were simply:

"Believe in yourself." "Don't be afraid to fail." and "It's not who you are, it's how you are."

These were the magic spells that got him through life whether he was on stage or with his family. And it was true, he didn't need any incantations to do what he did. He did everything he did because that's who he was. He didn't need or have any special superhuman powers.

But he was without a doubt a wizard.

THE PRESTIGE

Because making something disappear isn't enough; you have to bring it back. That's why every magic trick has a third act, the hardest part, the part we call "The Prestige".

Christopher Priest, The Prestige

Beyond the Velvet

by Michael Santiago

Venue upon venue, theaters sold out before ticket prices were disclosed. The time of entrepreneurial entertainers in Victorian England was at an all-time high. Some were high with the notion of fame. Others were drunk with it. But Salazar, stoic and steady, reached the pinnacle of the arcane within the breadth of four years--a notable feat for the inconsequential act of preplanned illusion. He never wavered or backed down at the alluring prospect of reaching the grand stage, The Mother Maiden. It welcomed only a few, yet it spun out even fewer elitists.

Demand often exceeded maximum occupancy. The grandiose interior was cobbled with silk curtains woven in Egypt, timber floors crafted by the Dutch, a stage designed from the French, and jade sculptures carved in China. The theater was an international display of fine exotic imports, and of colonialist might. Glamor struck the hall as guests poured in to see the next would-be wonder. Jesters, magicians, ventriloquists, musicians and cabaret dancers crowded the inner bowls backstage, waiting for their grand entrance to illicit resounding applause.

Among the hopeful, Salazar and his wife, Mina, tinkered with artifacts unique to their performance. They prepared as he anxiously awaited his name to be called to the center stage. Meanwhile, she began filling a four-meter-tall tank with water--the instrument for the grand finale. Turning to her husband, she said, "Do you really think we have a chance here? We are out of our league, and I am not even talking about the act. Look around."

An auspicious look took over, as he turned to his wife he said, "Mina, our act… our magic is going to transcend one's pigmentation and creed. With what I have concocted, they will forget that we even look different to them."

Interrupted by trumpets, the presenter regurgitated the

usual verbose introduction voice beyond the curtains yelled, "Gents, ladies, are you prepared to be blown right out of your seats? Brace, for we have a delectable line up of talented performers to pour through these halls. From Jesters, and yes, heckling is permitted, to those who manipulate the unexplainable. I am Taylor Smith, captain of this ship, and I welcome you to the grandest arena in all of England, The Mother Maiden."

Echoes of applause resounded throughout as the performers were making last minute adjustments to their act. Salazar, emboldened, raised his hand towards his face as a sliver of light escaped the main stage and shone on the pair. Momentarily using the spotlight, engorged by his wife's beauty, he snatched her in for a kiss, and said, "Do not worry. Tonight is where things take a turn for the better."

Taylor capitalized on his status as the premier host in all of Sussex. He reveled in it. The audience admired him for his dashing looks, tenacity, and charm. To him, he was Julius Caesar peering into his gladiatorial arena atop his podium. With more fame than those presenting, he often berated those lacking similar complexions or from far-off lands, and his felicitous quips never failed to give the crowd a spectacle.

Taylor sardonically stated, "Up next, we present a new face. One unlike any we were sure to see on this grand stage. Let him mystify you with unexplainable parlor tricks from the savage lands to the east. A land that will undoubtedly be gobbled up by our glorious matriarch soon enough. Without further ado, give a round of applause, if you'd like, for Salazar Hosseini, master of the Persian arts."

Tossing the satin velvet flaps aside, Salazar walked on stage and offered a pretentious bow to a displeased audience. Met with booing, he formed a gleeful grin and gestured for an assistant to accompany him. Mina rolled out a large, faux emerald chest. Reaching her hand inside, she pulled out a pair of finches from a brass wire cage.

Salazar grabbed one finch per hand, showing the onlookers that they were ordinary birds. Then, he clapped and rubbed his hands together as the audience bore a unifying grimace. Horrified by the act, a heckler shouted, "Is this what you primitive animals do where you're from?"

The crowd's response was unnerving, but he maintained the fluidity of his act and displayed both palms. Untainted by what appeared to be finch sacrifice, his hands were clean. Bewildered to what had happened, the attendees loosened up and looked on with curiosity.

As he started to hum a melancholic tune, he called for the two finches to reveal themselves. One beak, and then the second, prodded their way out of his top hat. They chirped and fluttered around the hall as Salazar began to grin. Pleased with the applause, he took a more genuine bow, and looked over to wink at his wife.

Grimace morphed to astonishment. The audience, hypnotized by the flitter of the finches, beckoned for more.

Salazar whispered into Mina's ear, "Honey, I think we can skip to the final act. The alternative one. You remember the protocol, don't you?"

"We haven't practiced that trick enough. What about that underwater disappearing act we planned for?" she suggested.

"Look at them. They are stupefied, mystified. We've yet to feed them a sliver and they are begging for more. We came to this stage to show them that they are wrong about us. Let us give them an act they'll never forget," he replied.

The begrudged presenter hesitantly began to clap, rallying the audience for another trick. "There we have it. A dazzling show of magic by the likes of these two. What say you, shall we have more?" Taylor yelled.

An unsatiated crowd began to shout for the show to continue. Grinning at the audience, Taylor tossed his left arm in the air and shouted, "Bravissimo, let's continue the show."

With a candid nod, Salazar urged Mina to get the instrument for the final act. She reached back into the emerald chest and clenched the grip of a howdah pistol. Handing the gun to Salazar, she paced backwards for five meters and stopped.

Salazar looked to the audience and raised the pistol with a firm grip. Bouncing his gaze throughout the hungry crowd, he said, "This is the resurrection. Two shots fired from this double barrel gun would be enough to dispatch even the most ferocious of beasts, but tonight, I will use this weapon on my wife. Do not be alarmed, for her death shall be temporary."

The plan was foolproof: load two blanks into the weapon and spin the illusion of death. She had two squibs filled with goat blood strapped to her chest. Both were connected to a pull string that would induce this murder mirage. And then, with a few phony incantations, she would rise and walk back over to her husband. Seemingly denying her passage down the river Styx. The audience would be none the wiser.

"Woah, woah, now Salazar, there is no need to slay your wife in front of these fine folk. Are you sure you two can't just settle for divorce?" Taylor quipped.

The audience chuckled, and Salazar said, "All good things must come to an end. Isn't that right, Mr. Smith?"

"A magic man and a comedian. We've got a special one here, folks," Taylor replied.

In an uproar, the crowd began chanting, "Take the shot. Take the shot."

As Salazar closed his eyes, the tension of the trigger tightened until the pop of two rounds exited the barrels. The act appeared to be a success. Mina fell right on cue and the goat blood pooled around her. She was so still; even managing to hold her breath to avoid any movement. He waved his hands in an irregular pattern and began reciting an ancient Parsi hymn intended to raise the dead. Clapping three times in a circular motion, he called for his wife to return to her body and rejoin the mortal realm, yet she didn't budge.

"It appears this Persian hocus pocus of yours needs a little fine tuning," Taylor chuckled.

Unamused, Salazar walked over to Mina and recited the passage again, yet nothing occurred. Still no breath. No movement. "Love, this isn't the time for this. We need to finish the act," he whispered. Tapping her forearm, he noticed the squibs still intact and that the blood was her own.

Shocked and terror-stricken, his mouth gaped, and his eyes became lifeless. Redirecting his gaze to the crowd, the harsh, blinding spotlights revealed that the trick had failed.

Taylor walked over to Salazar and whispered, "Pity, your magic didn't seem to work this time."

"Ladies and gents, there seems to be some technical difficulties, so an intermission is in order. Please, stock up on refreshments, light up a fag, and use the washroom. The show will recommence in fifteen minutes," Taylor said to the audience.

Kneeling before his wife, Salazar picked her up and began walking her breathless body off stage. However, before he could exit, Taylor tapped him on the shoulder and said, "Thank you. Now, get this savage bitch out of here. Oh, and before I forget, I don't know how you managed to con your way to this premiere, but you will not be stepping foot on any stage in Sussex. Let alone the whole of England. Magical man or not. Oh, and take your voodoo shit back to whatever hole you slithered out of."

A rebuttal eluded him, as his mind was preoccupied with the macabre, and of the words he uttered backstage minutes ago. With a deep gulp, he stumbled towards the exit. He was draped in disbelief; consumed by chagrin. Carrying the cadaver, he bellowed as his back collapsed against a wall. The weight of remorse grew heavier than the body. Staring into Mina's eyes, hollow, unoccupied eyes gazed back.

Unbeknownst to Salazar, he grieved adjacently to Taylor's dressing room. A muffled commotion could be heard from within.

He placed the body gently onto the ground and planted

his ear firmly against the dressing room door. The chatter became clear as he heard Taylor say, "Can you believe these people? Well, only one remains, and after tonight, he'll take himself and his dead bitch back to his desert land. Far from here. They have no place in this country, and never will. Just a shame we cannot do his grand act again. It's not like it took Sir Isaac Newton to replace the blanks with live rounds without anyone noticing."

"Replace the live rounds," Salazar repeated.

He jerked, backing away from the door, looking at his wife once more. Mortification morphed to menace swiftly. Now, riddled with scorn, he marched back to the stage to retrieve the pistol. Gleaning over the weapon, he tucked it into the left pocket of his lavender show coat; exiting the stage as trumpets signaled the end of intermission.

Faint steps in the distance grew louder as Taylor approached the velvet curtains. Brushing his hand in his hair with a pompous smirk, he stepped beyond the velvet with a grand gesture of self-importance. He flailed his hands in a flamboyant fashion as he pranced around the stage. The theater slowly repopulated as everyone began to find their seats. Taylor took a momentary pause from his shenanigans and shouted, "Please, everyone be seated. We have a wonderful show for you. Our next act will be delightful and disgusting. A French contortionist capable of dislocating every bone in his body. Under a mysterious guise, and an even stranger moniker. Everyone, welcome The Mandible to the stage."

The burly Frenchman walked on stage raising his arms in the air to hype the crowd. He placed one hand on his jaw and snapped it to the left. It hung in place bound by loose skin. Grotesque consumed the crowd as they looked on.

Backstage, Salazar scrambled to Taylor's dressing room. Rummaging through each drawer, he tossed the place upside down in pursuit of a single lead bullet. Behind the door, an idle coat rack had yet to be checked. Reaching into the side pocket, he pulled out a single round and loaded it into the pistol.

Sweaty palms clenched the ironclad grip as he exited the room.

On stage, The Mandible snapped every finger back into place with a spine tingling crack. He roared at the crowd, inciting applause for every bone popped. Masked with repugnance, Taylor joked, "Folks, I'm close to spewing breakfast."

Lingering behind the curtains, Salazar stormed the stage for one final act. Squinting down the sight, he aimed the pistol at Taylor and fired.

Taylor slowly drifted his view down to his abdomen and placed both hands onto his gut. Spewing blood over breakfast, he turned around to see Salazar lower the gun, and as he fell to his knees, he muttered, "You'll hang from the gallows, savage."

Peering into the audience, Taylor collapsed face first. As the blood pooled around him and the smoke from the barrel dissipated, the audience gave a standing ovation. Salazar turned to the crowd as they chanted for more.

As he squinted from the blinding rays of light from above, he began to wonder who the real savages were.

Synchrony
by Walter Moon

Zee felt the oxygen rush through her body as she began the Sim Go breathing technique. Her rapid breaths pumped her veins with life and jettisoned this newly invigorated blood throughout her internal depths. She felt her entire body. She silenced her mind completely. Everything that she controlled, utterly dedicated to the moment.

The moment split, ripping open the fabric of time and allowing her to enter another cosmic plane. In this plane, time was meaningless and ethereal. Moments passed over eons, and centuries ended with the snap of a finger.

Zee's being aligned.

Now complete, her consciousness stepped back through the portal, and into her corporeal body, as she exhaled her final breath of Sim Go. Zee opened her eyes, and set the arrow free from her taut bowstring. She closed her eyes again as the arrow soared up through the clouds, over the Floating Castle's parapets, between a crack in the keep's walls, arced down and slashed the kings throat, landing stiffly in the stone ground of the throne room as the despot bled out.

Marco Believed in Magic

by Lynette Esposito

Marco had schizophrenia. He thought he was magic. When he walked down the street and was in his normal state, he acted with kindness. He gave the few coins his sister gave to him, to the ones with signs that said "HUNGRY."

He wasn't hungry. At least not today. At breakfast, he had three eggs sunny side, five pieces of crisply fried bacon, four pancakes smothered in syrup and butter and one sausage. He would have had more sausages but the babies, little Melissa, five, and Derrick, four, liked them. His sister, big Melissa, loved it when he ate, so he ate as much as he could. No coffee, though. Coffee made him act crazy.

On Tuesday a week ago, he made multiple mistakes. The first mistake was that he drank one and a half cups of straight coffee. Then, he made a second mistake. He left home alone. That was the day he discovered how magical he was. He took off all his clothes except for his Hanes boxers. This was his third mistake. He would have been faster and not weighted down if he had taken off all of his underwear.

People gathered with cells phones raised like salutes. Do it, do it they chanted. He didn't know what they meant.

The police came and he hugged both of them. He knew them and they knew him.

They put their arms around him and led him to their police car. They were going to take him home.

The crowd chanted Leave him alone over and over. Marco smiled and waved. He bowed. He felt like a king.

I am magical he told Officer Jim. I know Jim nodded.

It started to drizzle. Marco shivered. He was sensitive to water. It made him feel afraid. Officer Dan patted his shoulder.

Me, too, he said. Water makes me nervous. Officer Dan looked over Marco's shoulder at the big bridge in front of them and shook his head

The crowd grew quiet. The sudden silence stunned Marko. He felt betrayed.

Everyone was looking at the bridge. A woman with a small girl waved back and forth. It appeared they were struggling. Then something flew downward into the water.

Marco felt his magic return. He shrugged free of Officer Dan. That little girl needed her dolly. He thought of little Melisa and big Melisa and he was off.

The water was cold. He moved on instinct plunging toward the dolly. His kept his breathing steady as he went under the bitter water. He had her or something. It was so light like a limp piece of water-soaked cloth.

He heard cheering as his head broke the water's surface and he took a deep magical breath sucking in all the air he could. A rope was lowered to him but it looked like a snake and he was afraid to take hold of it. The crowd chanted take it take it and his magic overcame his fear.

With one hand he grabbed the rope while with the other he held onto the wet cloth that dripped all over him as he was pulled free from the darkness around him.

The crowd went wild with glee as he handed the soaked fabric to Officer Jim who laid it on the ground and began kissing it. Odd Marko thought, a grown man kissing wet cloth.

Officer Dan put an arm around Marco and said Thatta Boy.

Someone in the crowd gave him a blue blanket to put on. It felt like a cape and it was warm.

Officer Jim looked up at the sky. Marco thought he saw Officer Jim's lips move. The paisley figure spurted some water and began moving. Officer Jim nodded and bowed his head.

The cloth sat up.

That's when Marco confirmed to himself that he was magical. The piece of cloth became a little girl. He did that. Marco raised his arms like Rocky in that old movie.

An ambulance arrived and the little girl was taken away. Officer Dan put his arm around Marko. I'll walk with you, he said. Let's get you home.

Five Seed Swindle
by Ryan Shane Lopez

From Jacob's Jack and the Beanstalk *& Christ's Parable of the*
Rich Man and Lazarus & others

There once lived a young prince who, after his five elder brothers had each met an untimely death and his father had fallen ill, took over the daily affairs of the kingdom. He placed a heavy burden upon his subjects and never lifted a finger to help even the least of them. By the fruit of their toil, the prince built for himself a splendid manor. Daily, he feasted sumptuously and clothed himself with fine purple linen, while his people fought against the ground.

One day, a peasant boy named Jimmy staggered up to the prince's gate, dragging behind him a white cow so thin that he had taken to using her ribs as a washboard. The boy sat at the gate and refused to leave until he spoke with the prince, no matter how the guards beat and threatened him. When at last the prince descended to the gate, holding a goblet of wine in one hand and gnawing on a leg of lamb with the other, the boy pleaded his case:

"Have mercy, my lord. My dear mother is sick and starving. We have no food and no family. Daily, I gather the crumbs from our neighbors' table for her to eat and chase away the dogs who come to lick her sores. This morning, she sent me to market and forbade me to return home until I sold this, our last milk cow. No one would buy her, for she no longer gives milk, but in your house she would surely grow fat and give milk again. Might you, who have riches to spare, give me five pounds for her?"

The prince had no need of cattle, but he had grown bored of late and decided to play a trick on the boy. Throwing the unfinished leg of lamb in the dirt, he reached into his purple robe and produced a small alabaster box. Opening it, he showed the boy five tiny seeds inside.

"Pounds, no," he said, "but I will swap you these five seeds."

A cloud passed over the boy's face.

"Fret not," continued the prince, "for these seeds were given me by my old governess who, between you and me, had some giant blood in her veins. If the stories she told were true, whosoever plants these seeds in the ground will never want for anything so long as they live. As you can see, I already want for nothing, so I will part with these enchanted seeds for your poor mother's sake."

Although his intentions were false, the prince's words were not entirely so. The governess had, in fact, given one seed to each of his elder brothers on the day they came of age, but had provoked his jealousy by giving him an alabaster box instead. After each untimely death, the prince had taken that brother's seed for himself. He had never believed his governess's stories, however, for the old bitty's mind had been as wobbly as a loose wagon wheel. Besides, he saw no reason for keeping the seeds now that everyone who knew their significance was dead.

Jimmy, who was still young enough to believe in fairy tales, snatched up the alabaster box and ran home to tell his mother of their good fortune.

Some time after, Jimmy returned to the prince's gates. When the prince went down to meet him, Jimmy handed him a single gold coin, the purity of which he had never seen.

"How did you come by this, boy?" asked the prince.

The boy told this story:

"When I showed my mother the seeds you gave me, she chided me from dusk until midnight. Since we had nothing else, we ate the seeds for dinner. We had two apiece, but I could not find the fifth and judged it must have fallen out as I ran. The next morning, Mother sent me to town to sell the alabaster box. Along the way, I crossed through a neighbor's field and noticed a mustard tree which had not been there before. Already it came up to my chin and appeared to grow taller every second. I went straight to the owner of that field, who sold it to me for the alabaster box and our cottage and all we owned. Then, I fetched Mother and took her to live beneath the mustard tree, which by then stood as tall as a house and was growing still.

"On the third morning, the treetop tickled the underbelly of passing clouds and whole flocks of birds nested in its branches. Curious, I began to climb and even as I climbed it grew. At its highest point, I discovered a magnificent castle floating among the clouds. From the castle gates, I saw a woman arrayed in a dress which shone like the sun and a twelve-pointed crown which glittered like starlight. On her hands and knees, she was searching the castle courtyard by the light of her dress (for I had climbed so long that night had fallen). I called to the shining woman and when she came to the gate, I saw she must be a head taller than the tallest man alive."

At this, the prince recoiled, for he knew this woman to be his old governess, who had died by his hand after accusing him of murdering his brothers.

"The shining woman had lost a coin and she invited me in to help her search for it," Jimmy continued. "When I found it, she rejoiced by hosting a feast in her banquet hall and sitting me at the head of her table. The hall and the food and the guests were all so divine that I could not paint their beauty if ten thousand poets' tongues were my brushes, but I would trade all my days in this world for but another hour at that splendid table. Afterward, the shining woman gave me not one but ten gold coins, more than enough to build my mother a new cottage and care for her properly. I offer you one of these coins now for the kindness you have shown my mother and me."

The prince accepted the coin with humility in his mouth and envy in his heart, scheming how he might gain for himself the riches of the floating castle. Yet he dared not climb the tree, for he feared the giantess in the sky more than any man or beast upon the earth.

"Will you climb the mustard tree again?" he asked young

Jimmy. "Surely, the lady of the castle would be pleased to hear how you have used her gift to provide for your poor mother."

Jimmy, in his awe and wonder, had forgotten to mention his mother to the giantess and agreed he should visit her again if only to express his gratitude.

Three days later, he returned to the prince's estate. This time, he brought with him a pearl of inestimable value. He claimed that on hearing of his mother's condition, the shining woman had given him a golden oyster which would produce such a pearl anytime he asked for one. The pearl so enamored the prince that he offered the boy everything he owned in exchange for it.

"It is already yours," said the boy, "for the kindness you have shown my mother and me."

"Heaven knows no gratitude like yours," flattered the prince, though he believed the golden oyster to be his by all rights. He might have arrested the boy and seized all his possessions then and there, but he wanted to see what other treasures his old governess might be hoarding. "I had hoped the shining woman would have provided a remedy for your mother's ailments. Surely, it is not beyond her power to ease the suffering of the afflicted."

Seeing the wisdom of the prince's words, Jimmy agreed to climb the tree a third time.

After three more days, the boy returned with a vial of sparkling rainwater which the shining woman had drawn from a well in the first cloud God ever made. This water, which had never once touched the earth, was so pure that one drop had not only healed his mother but had restored all the vitality and beauty of her bygone youth.

"It is yours," said the boy, offering the vial to the prince. "I want for nothing now. May you show all your subjects the same kindness you have shown my mother and me."

The prince saw within reach his deepest desires: the

unending wealth of the golden oyster and the unending health of the virgin rainwater. He needed only to rid himself of Jimmy and the mustard tree, for the prince was not content to only have these treasures for himself, but needed to ensure no one else, not a soul but himself, ever got close to them.

"Now that she is well," he said, "will you take your mother to meet her benefactor in the sky?"

This idea thrilled young Jimmy, for he longed to share the wonders of the floating castle with his beloved mother, and he ran off to tell her.

The next morning, the prince went to the giant mustard tree, which was not hard to find since it could be seen from anywhere in the kingdom. As expected, the boy had taken his mother up the tree and left unattended the cottage he'd built at its base. The prince went in and stole the remaining gold coins and the enchanted oyster. Then he summoned his father's soldiers, about a thousand in all, armed them with freshly sharpened axes, ordered them to chop down the mustard tree, then bind its stump with iron and bronze. After a day and a night of chopping, the great tree came crashing down, crushing to dust all but 144 of the soldiers.

Back at his manor, the prince asked the golden oyster for a pearl, but it would not open. He asked in every combination of tone and words he could imagine, but it would not open. He asked in every foreign language he could speak, but still it would not open. Day after day, he pleaded for a pearl until he grew so frustrated that he tried to pry open the oyster with his fingers. It slipped and sliced deep cuts into both his hands. Enraged, the prince drew his sword and smashed the oyster with its hilt. Shards of the golden shell flew up and lodged in his face. Crying out in pain, he took out the vial of virgin rainwater and drank.

But he was not healed.

The golden shards in his face grew larger and lodged themselves deeper into his flesh, even into his bone. The cuts in his hands filled up with gold, which hardened so that he could not close his fists. He dropped the vial, shattering it against the stone floor. Desperate to ease his pain, he fell to his knees to lap up the rainwater which, having touched the ground, had lost its purity.

Just then, the prince heard the clamor of voices and, looking out his window, saw a mob of angry peasants approaching his gate. He had under his command now only 144 soldiers, whose loyalty was waning fast. Seeing that his gates would not long overcome the mob, the prince escaped through a secret passage and fled to his father's castle.

But he found no help there. On seeing his son's hideous appearance, the king cursed him. Furthermore, on hearing of the rainwater which might have healed him had the prince not kept it for himself, the king had his son stripped of his crown and purple linens before casting him out.

Disowned and disfigured, the former prince sat among the beggars outside the castle gates. When the people saw him there, they overpowered him, dug their fingers into his flesh, and ripped the gold from his face and hands. No matter how much gold they tore out, it always grew back and the pain of the tearing and regrowth was unbearable. So the once rich and powerful prince fled the town and wandered seven years alone in the wilderness, filling his belly with the grass of the field and quenching his thirst with the dew of heaven.

One day, seeking refuge, he returned to the mustard tree. Although it had fallen, its leaves and branches had continued to flourish, producing thousands of seeds and giving shelter to the birds of the air and the beasts of the field. There he found the boy's white cow, which he had let loose to starve in the wilderness, now grown fat off the leaves of the mustard tree. Longing to fill his aching belly, the former prince tried to milk the cow, but could not close his hands around her teats. So he tried to suckle from the cow like a newborn babe, but the shards protruding from his face cut the cow's teat and she ran away.

Humiliated, he wept and cried out to the heavens, asking that he might die.

In reply, he heard echoing through the clouds a joyous and full-hearted laughter. Listening, he recognized the voice of the peasant boy, Jimmy, joined by a second voice which must be his mother's. He called out, asking them to remember his kindness to them and send help.

The clouds parted and his old governess appeared to him as a shining giantess.

"They cannot hear you," her voice thundered. "They are at home in my halls now, where they enjoy every happiness and comfort."

"Have mercy, my lady," pleaded the former prince, "for I am in anguish. Let Jimmy draw a cup of the virgin rainwater and lower it down to me, that I might drink and be healed."

"The distance is too great," she called down. "He has no rope nor anything else long enough to reach you and you have cut down the mustard tree, the only bridge between here and there. But even if you drank of the virgin rainwater, it would not grant you the relief you seek, for rain makes grow only that which already dwells in the soil and a seed can only sprout what it already contains. Within the boy's mother there had survived a measure of youth and beauty, so that one drop of the water caused that youth and beauty to grow and fill her whole being until there remained no room for the roots of sickness. But the soil of your heart has gone bad, for you have spent your days cultivating nothing but greed and selfishness."

"If you will not help me, then help my father, who will surely regain his health now that I am longer there to dose his meals with poison. I beg you, send the boy to warn him against the folly of greed and arrogance."

"I tell the truth, if he will not learn from your example, then he will not listen even if a voice speaks to him from the heavens."

Then, the shiny lady vanished among the clouds and spoke to him no more.

Heroes and Villeins

by Desiree Ducharme

It was a terrible misunderstanding that started with a misspelling. Knowing you are the victim of vocabulary is of little comfort or redress when you are chained to the wall of a dungeon awaiting your pyre. Knowledge does not sate your hunger. It does not ease the aching cold in your bones or soothe the burns on and beneath your skin. Truth does not stay the hand that holds the hot poker or dull the pain in your ruined, nail-less digits. Your mother always told you words had power, which is why reading is forbidden, but you didn't listen. You ignored her words and set off to find your own. Now she is dead. Your father is dead. Your farm was burnt to the ground and you are soon to follow. All because of a book and a regional spelling variant.

Facts are of little consolation when your life dangles at the end of a chain. You did not lie during your coerced confession. You told them everything. Well, you told them what an illiterate villein's girl-child would tell old men pressing hot metal into her skin. In short, whatever would make them stop.

You told them how you found it, tangled in the remains of the old rowan tree. The Lord had recently returned from a murder spree on the continent. He issued a new edict requiring all rowan trees be removed from his lands.

You were following orders. You told them how you thought it was a rock after you broke the ax head upon it. You scream the story of your mother burning it with the rest of the midden as they peel the skin from the bottom of your feet. Sobbing through tears, you tell them how it did not burn. They placed your skinless soles over hot coals. You could smell yourself roasting as you told them how your father threw it in the lake. You salivate and cry out the truth. You don't know how it ended up in the belly of the eel. You rush to tell them how you brought it directly to the Heroes of the Holy Order as the stones slowly compress and fracture your ribs.

"You are a family of villains!"

"Yes, villeins, peasants! We know nothing of books and live to serve our great and noble Lord!"

"See, confession is good. Your soul is saved."

"I care not for my soul, what of my life? And my parents?"

"You are blasphemous villains, your lives are forfeit."

"No, we're villeins not villains. Please, we've done no wrong. We followed the Lord's edict. We burned it, we drowned it. When that didn't work, I brought it to you, the Heroes. We found it, but we are loyal villeins!"

"That's what I said."

"Villeins. With an e not an a!"

"What strange magic you try. Spelling will not save your life."

"My parents have done nothing wrong."

"Your parents are no more. You clearly know how to spell, which means you can read. Reading is a dangerous thing, especially for a girl, and dangerous things need burning. Be content, your soul belongs to God once more. Your body will be cleansed by fire and returned to the earth." The Hero's tone was flat and factual, his words far more injurious than sharp hot metal could ever be.

You did not tell them how the gnarled roots opened like fingers at your touch. Even as they pulled your fingernails out, the sensation of the roots moving under your palms kept this detail from your tongue. You failed to mention the wrappings. How you'd never seen skins like them and could not imagine the creatures they came from. Even after what must have been centuries in the earth, they were shiny as though recently oiled and buffed. How they sparkled like liquid gems in the grey dusk. How they slipped apart revealing the rowan tree embossed on the cover of the tome.

You did not tell them how supple the binding was. How the day's labor pains were drawn out of you as you traced the tree on the front. How the knowledge of the Universe flowed into you. Through seven days of being picked apart by holy heroes, these details stayed locked away. You are strangely comforted by this thought. You feel your mother would be proud.

Your father did throw it in the lake. This was not a lie. It washed up on the shore the next day. He rowed to the very center, tied several rocks to it, and dropped it in. You pulled it from your well three days later, rocks, rope and all. Your mother panicked and tossed it into the river.

Several days later, you bring home an eel from the market. Your parents did not see the eel's skin pucker, stretch and reveal the pattern of the rowan tree at your touch. They did not witness the eel's exposed vertebrae widen and darken as you pulled the skin off. They did not watch as flesh and bone became pages, boards, and spine. Perhaps if they'd been there you would not have opened it. Doesn't really matter now.

They found you in the field at dawn, naked and covered in viscera. A ring of seven rowan saplings around you. One tree for each year of your life. Your father pulled the saplings. He burned them. Like the book, they did not burn. He tied them to rocks, rowed to the center of the lake, and dropped them in.

Your mother dresses you in a new cloak and a pair of new boots. She tells you to go into the forest to find mushrooms. She tells you to avoid rowan trees. She asks if you can read. You nod. You are both crying.

"They cannot take that from you. It is part of you. This life is filled with dark places. You will never be alone but you will be lonely. You must choose your words. They are powerful. Be wary of heroes, they embrace a single purpose and resist correction. Tell no one of the saplings. Now, run."

You met your Hero where the road crossed Hadrian's wall.

He warns you of the dangers of traveling alone. He tells you he was a villein once and the Order saved him and made him a hero. He smells of smoke and what you now know to be burning human flesh. He is the one who takes you to the Order. He lights the fires that produce the coals for your torture. Each night, he visits you and feeds you. He tells you of his life, how he lost his wife and child to plague. How the Order gave him purpose in hunting down villains.

You ask how many people he has killed. You point out the spelling error. He is resistant to correction. He begs for your life on the seventh day. He wraps the cloak around you before they tie you to the stake. He is crying, but you are not.

"I am sorry, child. I could not save you."

"Leave the Order. There is still time for you to save yourself. I gather they will need villeins to work the land now that my parents are dead. It would bring me comfort to know you served our Lord in their place. You could visit me in the lake."

"You are a strange child."

"What can I say, I am a villain. You can save me by adding rowan branches to my pyre. Even if you do not, I forgive you." You kiss his bowed head. He tucks your hair under the hood of your cloak. You think of your father as your Hero adjusts your cloak so it envelops all of you. You are comforted by this small kindness. His eyes are so like your mother's when she told you to run. "Go now, Hero. This dangerous thing needs burning."

Fun fact: even atop the pyre, you notice the smoke first. It is the smoke that fills your lungs and takes your breath. It is smoke that robs the Heroes of the Holy Order of your screams. The smoke steals you away to unconsciousness as the flames dance. You do not see your Hero add the rowan branches. He does. He has replaced all the Mercy Sticks with rowan branches. Your pyre burns hot and loud. They cannot put it out. The stone beneath it melts. All the trees within Holy Keep burn from the roots upward.

The smoke from your pyre blocks the sun for seven days.

The flames from your pyre light the square for seven nights. The keep is abandoned. Your Hero tells your story to the villeins. He writes it down. He distributes copies of it. He corrects the spelling error next to your name in the Order's records. He gathers all the un-burnt rowan into a bundle and takes it with him when he leaves.

Rowan trees spring from the ashes where you burned. They grow quick and hard. Within a few months, the keep is overwhelmed by a forest of rowan. The Heroes of the Holy Order are recalled to their palaces of gilt and glory. Your Hero returns to the farm where he murdered your parents. He buys the fallow land from your erstwhile Lord. At the center of the lake, there is now an island surrounded by seven rowan trees.

In the village, he learns that the island erupted from the lake in a column of smoke and flame that blocked the sun for seven days and lit the sky for seven nights. No one goes out on the lake anymore. There is no life within it save the rowan trees. The villagers tell him a legend of a woman condemned. A legend filled with Heroes and Villains. A legend of dangerous knowledge that cannot be taken only given or found within yourself. Of a sorceress reborn from the ashes of rowan trees and forgiveness.

He goes there to visit you. He places the bundle of un-burnt rowan in the center of the island, and beneath it, a copy of your story which he has had illuminated.

He lights the pyre at midnight during the summer solstice. He weeps for you and for those he killed. He collects his tears. In the morning, he waters the ashes with them. He works the land and keeps to himself.

When an eighth tree appears, the Hero-turned-villein rows to the island.

Magic Act
by David James Poissant

The magician is having trouble reassembling his assistant.

The trick is one he's done hundreds of times before. The assistant goes in. The saw goes through. The boxes are elevated waist-high like gurneys on wheeled stilts. The boxes spin, and the assistant kicks her feet. The boxes are brought back together. The lids lift, and the assistant rises, smiling, in one piece.

Only, this time, when the lids lift, the assistant is not in one piece. The assistant is two halves, separated at the waist, as with an invisible belt.

There is no blood, no gore. The assistant cannot feel a thing. It's only when she looks down that her smile drops. She looks to him.

"Keep smiling," the magician whispers, then shuts the lids. "Let's try that again!"

The audience laughs generously.

The magician spins the boxes harder this time. The assistant's blonde hair is a comet. A shoe clatters to the stage.

The magician brings the boxes together again. Again he lifts the lid.

Same halves. Same invisible belt.

"Third time's the charm!" the magician shouts.

The audience laughs less generously.

The magician flings the boxes so hard one collides into the gold-fringed curtain and the other almost rolls offstage.

The boxes are brought back together. The magician wipes his brow. The audience murmurs its concern.

The magician lifts one lid and peers inside. The assistant is definitely still cut in half.

The magician shuts the box, taps each lid twice with his magic wand.

The wand's a good one, pro model, real wood, black with chrome tips. When it comes to magic, the magician spares no expense.

For good measure, the magician taps the assistant's toes, and, gently, the assistant's narrow brow.

The assistant shuts her eyes.

She is not his wife, though the magician gets that question a lot. Not a girlfriend. He is old enough to be her father, though she is not his daughter, not a relative of any kind. She is his employee.

The magician is a good employer, fair. He pays the assistant biweekly. Every six months, he buys her a new uniform. Each year, he issues her a W-2. Together, their LLC has survived two recessions, four rabbits, and more doves than the magician can count. Together, he and the assistant have survived three unruly crowds, two fires, and a dangerous bout of swine flu. The assistant has survived 934 counts of being sawn in half.

"Presto change-o," the magician incants, though he hasn't used an incantation in years, not since Gerald over at Lights, Camera, Magic! LLC stole his catchphrase: "From heavens high and regions nether, put this woman back together!" It wasn't a good incantation, but it was his, until it wasn't.

Gerald.

Gerald with his website and podcast and check mark on Twitter. Gerald with his two assistants.

The magician flings open the lids. The woman remains cut in half.

"Boo!" an audience member yells, and a chorus of boos

fills the air.

The magician does not know what comes next. Should he call the authorities? Should he call another magician? He's not calling Gerald, that's for sure.

The audience boos loudly. One family leaves, the mother covering her young son's eyes.

In the front row, a man raises a phone to snap a picture. Others follow. Soon, everyone is too busy taking pictures to boo.

"I'm sorry," the magician says. "I'm so sorry."

The assistant will not open her eyes.

The audience will not leave. They crowd closer, gawking, angling, all elbows and phones.

The assistant opens her eyes. "Let me out."

"But your legs," the magician says.

"Let me out. Let me out."

The magician raises one lid, then the other. He lowers the assistant's legs to the floor.

Her bottom half wobbles, as though the waist works a hula hoop. Then the feet find their footing, and the legs depart stage left into the wings.

The magician cradles the assistant's top half, pulling the assistant from the box.

What will he tell the woman's parents? Her children?

What will he tell the police?

The magician is ruined. His license will be stripped from him, his magic hat impounded, and wand revoked. He'll never practice magic in the lower forty-eight again.

Perhaps he can find work in Italy. He has a cousin there.

Or a second cousin. He can't remember which.

But now is not the time to think of Italy. For, even now, the assistant's top half is being torn from the magician's arms. And now the audience is on her, snapping selfies, passing her around.

By evening, pictures of the magician's assistant will fill Instagram. By morning, she will be a meme. Next week, she'll inspire three TikTok dances, and, by next year, the magician's assistant will host her own late night network show.

The magician will not be one of her guests. The assistant will never speak to the magician again.

"Give her back to me," the magician calls from the stage. "Bring her back!"

The audience-turned-crowd ignores him. The assistant ignores him.

Tentatively, the assistant's legs peek out from behind the curtain, then charge forward. They kick the magician in the shins.

The magician stuffs his wand and hat into his bag.

He is forgotten.

Already, the crowd chants the assistant's name. Already, that name is trending on Twitter.

The magician could call Gerald, beg him for a job.

But no. A magician who cannot reassemble his assistant is no magician. He's just a man with a dove in his pocket, a man in a tuxedo with two boxes and a saw.

The magician releases the dove from his pocket. The bird flies over crowd, but the people take no notice. Cameras flash. The assistant smiles for the phones. The bird swoops and dives, and then the bird is gone.

My Father, the Villain
by Eric Thralby

My father was attacked by an unidentified animal. It concentrated on his eyes and neck. He is horrible to look at.

He has become an angry threat because of his deformity. When people look, he looks back. When people ask, he follows them into the store and harasses them until they leave. Our graduation rate plummets because children are terrified and refuse to go to school. Our mortality rate among the old skyrockets because of the safety in death.

We begin to worry he's become too aggressive, myself, my brother, and our two sisters and mother.

We buy him a mask and bring him to a mirror to try it on. We massage his shoulders and pat his arms and encourage him with every sound we know. He stands as indifferent as a pile of rocks and pulls the mask on.

'What is it?' he says.

'It is a magical mask,' I say. 'It will instantly make you OK.'

He turns side to side, feeling the mask, looking close in the mirror as if shaving. Even under a magical mask, my father is as hideous as ever.

He pulls it off and walks past us and leaves his mask on the counter.

I cannot say for sure where he goes, but I can guess as to his usual haunts: the pet adoption center, any daycare within radius, and, he has done it before, live television via the broadcasting tower.

The mask remains on the counter for weeks. Our father has become more and more, since the animal attack, a lump of putty, a pitiable man with always a handful of pebbles, and a heart full of hate. Whenever he stands up to leave, he stares us down until we recoil from his face. And then he slams the door and runs.

'But what will we do? Our mother has become a wreck and our father a plague.'

We sit on our couches and drink. I fumble the instructions, which I have taped back together, for the magical mask in my hands and read for my brother and sisters: 'Welcome to the magical mask. If indeed the mask is no good, try encouraging words. Again, if this is to no effect, believe in the magic of gloves and a belt, among other accessories of choice. With love, from magic, the magical mask.'

'This helps nothing,' says my sister, who is tickling our sister to share the Kahlua.

I'll show you, I think silently, clenching my hands and crumbling the paper. I realize then that I am just like my father. I go to my bed in a cold sweat of terror.

The next morning, the magical mask is cockeyed on the counter. A pair of gloves, red and black, almost sinister, yet powerful, tucked beneath the magical mask.

At lunch our father returns to his chair, his knuckles tattooed and holding a bag full of money. I skip out of lunch and buy a red and black cape from the costume store. As the Kahlua comes out and I go to tuck the cape under the magical mask with the gloves, I see already there is a pair of red boots with black laces and streaks that light up.

Under cover of night, when we siblings are not enough drunk and considering more, we go to the phone and see it has all disappeared: the cape, the boots, the gloves, the magical mask and our rotten father.

We turn on the television and flip to the news.

'Heinous!'

'Diabolical!'

'Incomparably EVIL!'

Our father hovers above a burning building, his red and black cape fluttering handsomely in the wind. He stares into the camera.

We have healed him, our father. And now he is the world's concern.

That shallow, musty grey, almost stagnant creek

by Shireen Arora

People warned that the creek was magical
yet none could describe the sorcery of it
people warned that the creek in the forest was magical
but magic is not real
it's a supposition to frighten children,
a myth created by people
a surmise woven by folklore
certainly not real.

People warned that the shallow, musty grey creek was magical
but the only thing that looked special were the rocks
rocks as far as the eye could see
lining the creek
porous coral rocks and ancient, stratified rocks and solid crustal
rocks and grey, rough-cut rocks,
moss-covered rocks and glass-like jagged rocks and slippery flat
rocks and sunbaked brown rocks.

People warned that the almost stagnant creek was magical
but magic is not real
so I leaped over the creek
hopped over the rocks
danced as I mocked the notion
of the creek with magical abilities.
But what happened next is lost in history
I slowly started to vanish. From my toes to
my ankles to my shins to my knees
to my thighs to my
body to my arms
to my neck to
my chin
to my
ears
nose
and

then
to
my
eyes.

It felt like I was falling.
My body, stock-still.
My arms merged with my torso. My eyes cemented to my face.
Finally the realization hit me
I had turned into a rusty red rounded rock.
Devoured by the magic of the creek.
And now I whisper my warning to the trees, the birds, the frogs,
the air, the wind, the sun, the clouds, anyone who listens.
The creek is magical.

Tiny Babbitt
by Rachel Aydt

Beth Babbitt's parents died after an airplane slid off the runway in Chicago because of ice buildup. By the time they were gone, she was already grown, living alone in a floor-through apartment in downtown Manhattan. All there was to do was call the family lawyer. There was no funeral, because her parents were incinerated, and no elders remained to care for her. There was no memorial service because she never paid attention to who should have come. She was an only child, and after they died, no one sought out her company or inquired into her well-being. She never felt close to her parents, and they never seemed particularly close to one another. This ambient distance between them spilled over into her developing life. As a teenager, she didn't feel beholden to the intense friendships that adorned most girls around her; she was happier in her own company. Despite this, she imagined herself as a mother one day, but understood with a solemn clarity, that she could do better than her own. Her parents had failed, in so many ways. They were too oblivious to observe the rituals that dotted the other childhoods around her. If her father's career were a silent filmstrip, a briefcase would open and close, over and over again; his back would be turned away from the camera, his mouth moving into the phone, his hand wrapped around the coiled phone wire. If her mother were a silent filmstrip, she would be glamorous, a dutiful socialite, always bouncing around a circuit of hair appointments and tea dates with everyone but her own child.

And so, it wasn't much of a stretch, the before and after of her orphan status. For a time, she carried a sort of grief at the full weight of being alone in the world, the hollow ark of a consciousness. Even the small touchstones—the newspaper, the coiled phone cord, the tea dates, and the silence between them, erased in a moment. Their erasure was disorienting—the lack of warmth, after all, leaves a chill. Even in the heat of her parents burned to bits.

*

Although she couldn't see the stars in the hampered darkness of the city nights, Beth thought a lot about the cosmos. Certain words could hit her ear and send her into a daydream. Ziggy *Stardust*; *dwarf planets, dark matter, entropy.* "Space is a hard vacuum, meaning it is a void containing very little matter," she once read in a magazine. At least some of the little matter was comprised of her parents. They were transformed after having lived out their cold and suburban life cycles.

And what of Beth's life cycle? She understood she was spun into the destiny of the cyclical nature of the physical world. She began to crave companionship. She had never been one to pick men up at bars; did people even do that anymore? Instead, she went on a couple of online dates, but found men a bother. They spoke too fast, skating across things she didn't care the slightest bit about. They were divorced; they struggled with taking care of themselves; they complained. Eventually, this tedious cycle wound its way toward another solution. She could skip the relationship altogether. And so, instead, she found a sperm donor.

"Give Life to Your Dream" the website splashed across the homepage. A popup ad offered 15% off of all sperm straws. *We're celebrating our 30-year anniversary and want to give you something to celebrate too! Browse your perfect donor today!* Their names were alphabetical. Abner and Ace and Ahab; Gerard and Gilroy. Patton and Sergio. Ace was an actor; Stig was a student of aerospace engineering. Ahab included a childhood photograph of himself leaning over a tricycle in what appeared to be a cool climate, his red wool cap barely containing a head full of curly black hair. Call me Ahab! Beth clicked the baby carriage icon next to his photo, which led her to the shopping cart. After ponying up $791 US dollars, baby Ahab hit the postal system. But first, she had to select a shipping method. "If it is difficult to predict your ovulation date, we recommend you select a nitrogen tank. We do not recommend dry ice shipments over the weekend."

When Tiny Babbitt was born on the 9th floor of St. Vincent's Hospital on Lower Manhattan, he yawned his way out of Beth's belly through a 5-inch incision, right above her pelvic bone. For the first few hours, hers was a labor as on-time as an English railroad clock. Then, an interruption to the smooth ebbs and flows of the contractions; blood pressure of mother and child dropped, and a snap decision from her doctor brought her from labor room to surgical suite, bright lights and masks and curtains and hushed urgency. Tangles of nerves were numbed by a skilled anesthesiologist who gave a spinal tap. Then, layers of dermis cut through completely by cesarean, and a mere sensation around her waist of a belt being pulled tight. A few moments later, a tiny face, open eyes and peach colored skin, still wet from the place he'd cocooned. Beth shivered, as from a flu, sensitive to every touch, bump, and sound.

"There you are. You're so tiny," she said when the doctor held him near her so she could see. He wasn't *really* tiny. He was 21-inches long in fact, and weighed 7 pounds and 6 ounces, more than a bright yellow sack of Domino sugar and bigger than most Purdue roasters. Wrapped in the hospital issue flannel, with pink and blue stripes, his giant eyes belied the rest of his head, and in that moment, he owned his name. They were alone then. The clattering of surgical tools in metal bowls receded; the din of voices blended into a deep hum of relief.

Rituals of a warm motherhood, systematically withheld from her as a girl, came easily. When Tiny lost a tooth, Beth stopped off at a subway machine to get gold dollars to slip under his pillow. When it was St. Patrick's Day, she drummed up netted sacks of gold chocolate coins at the corner deli and put them in the middle of the living room, along with a trail of green glitter that led to a window. "Wake up Tiny, the Leprechaun came!" Tiny hung on to her long black hair and shared the chocolate with her that every Bunny and Leprechaun and Santa Claus left on their apartment's doorstep. He made tea parties and let her have the first poured cup. On the one hand, he was turning into a little gentleman. On the other, he existed in his space like a thousand snapping rubber bands.

*

Tiny bent down to tie his shoes for the third time after his teacher, Ms. Eileen, implored him to *get it right this time*. The first time was in morning meeting. "Tiny Babbitt, stop trailing your laces and *get with the program*." The second time was at morning recess. Making his way up the ladder of the blue plastic slide, she was shrill and to the point. "Tiny Babbitt! Tiny Babbitt! Tie that shoe!" It's true; his lace did dangle, grey and chewed up at the ends where once pristine. Her voice slid over him as it had so many times before, and as many other voices had before hers. On the playground; at a playdate; in the pediatrician's office. Despite the vague sense of vertigo at the top step of the slide, he teetered, reached for the offending lace, and tucked it into his shoe.

*

Tiny had a penchant for hair. *He'll be the next Frédéric Fekkai*, Beth quipped on the playground to other parents with toddlers, on afternoons tense from too much touching and grabbing. His little fingers sought every strand of hair in his wake and dragged across any surface that rendered his fingernails filthy. From head to toe his body was laced with slumbering nerves that needed more input to feel. It was like he'd been born with calluses over his entire skin, and in order to reach tactile sensations he had to reach much, much further. Banging trucks in sandboxes. Eating sand. Flinging himself from the monkey bars. Other mothers were far more fastidious than she was. Sandboxes were highly anxious helicoptering zones. Children who grabbed toy trucks from another were swiftly scolded; hand sanitizer bottles were squeezed every five minutes. Eventually she stopped trying to socialize him altogether. When they were at home, Tiny tugged on her hair like an orangutan baby. Her scalp grew tender to the touch, but she couldn't bear to make him stop.

*

The crack in the connection between Beth and Tiny was imperceptible before it wasn't. In his quirky ways, Tiny was thriving, but his childhood was leeching out whatever strength Beth had left in her. Other parents, she observed, were able to shoulder the layers of responsibilities. As a list, the routine was feasible: go shopping, cook a little something, clean up, tend to personal hygiene and doctors' appointments, take Tiny to and from school, be a part of a community, even if hanging on the periphery. She was so lucky, she knew, that she didn't have to worry about money like so many other parents, like so many other single mothers. Still, the weight of the manageable pile grew unmanageable. The crack widened; depression had found her. It was like they were swimming in the middle of an ocean, and there was one life raft, and it was thrown to Tiny. There were times when she knew they couldn't both make it; when she wouldn't be able to join him when he reached land.

These schisms were seasonal, ticking off the calendar like clockwork. It was a paralysis settling over her every few months, a grey wool forming over her eyes, and then mouth, and then body. Her wings fell off and she moved backwards into a cocoon, leaving Tiny to care for himself. This was confusing: overnight, his mother went from loving and tolerant and buoyant to catatonic and incapable of performing even the most basic tasks. All day and into the night, Beth laid down on the couch as he sat at her curled-up feet, looking at picture books with animated characters. A cat dressed like a pirate conquered a threatening ship, a skull flag hanging from its mast. Or, a cedar forest, soft with lichen-dotted trees and paths where vulnerable children walked deeper and deeper into a forest, holding hands. He would get to the eighth page and put it down before the witch opened the door to the cottage.

*

At six years old, Tiny was learning to take care of himself. He made peanut butter and jelly sandwiches, letting sticky globs of fruit land on the kitchen floor, where Beth left them to dry. Her hair grew tangled. His clothes grew dirty. It was all she could do to put him on the bus in the mornings, his little eyes blinking back at her through the window of the "half cheese" school bus. Beth couldn't stand how lethargic she'd become. Tiny would walk her toothbrush over to her at night and give her an empty soup can to spit in. He would play Beauty Shop and attempt to comb out her tangled hair while she sat catatonic on her couch. He would even walk to the corner deli with five dollars in his pocket to pick up a quart of milk and a few bananas. The cashier's grave mistake was thinking this was charming.

In other ways, Tiny wasn't as clear about his needs. When he was hungry, his stomach offered that insight, and he could follow it like the sound of a hollow drum. But other parts of his days suffered: action figures played alone, not with one another; rooms were quiet, not filled with music; cavities took root in his emerging molars, despite his brushing. He stared into his neighbor's windows at night. He watched planes fly overhead, little specks of dark leaving streaks of smoke in their wake. And when his eyes were sated, he would turn around to his mother once again, and offer something substantive, like a word or two, or a banana. "You're my little gentleman," she would coo, and his cup would spill over.

When he needed attention, he learned to throw himself into furniture over and over again, the thwack on his little body resonating as affection. The harder he slammed, the better he felt. At the worst times, Beth would stretch out her arms and attempt to block him. "Why are you doing that? What's the matter with you?" and the answer to that question was another deep slam into a surface. Afterward his relief was palpable. Were he an eraser, there would be no residual chalk dust left to clap on the sidewalk.

*

The cocoon would split, eventually. It always did. The musty edges of the grey pallor that covered Beth's world began to loosen their grip. With an instinct to self-preserve, she pulled out an old camera and began to leave the apartment to take pictures along the East River promenade. Her subjects were often bridges, or waterfowl that slipped in and out of the shimmering surface, squiggling fishes in their beaks. Watching the doomed fish meet their fate, she imagined her life in the animal world.

She was more insect than amphibian. An insect with stages: egg, larva, pupa, adult. She'd morphed into her adult stage, and with that came a set of delicate wings. Flying ants, she read, were the only ones to reproduce, using their wings to swarm and mate.

Tiny learned to sit on the sidewalk with a magnifying glass and hold them up to light where the ants would march, in the grassy seams of the broken concrete. When he tilted the glass just so, the beam halted an ant in its tracks until it curled into itself and smoked. The other ants would walk around the flecks of remains, moving in wavy snake-shaped patterns.

*

She got her film developed at the photography counter at Walgreens. The pimpled kid behind the register began to recognize her. "Here you go, matte, not glossy," he said, handing her back the latest batch of two-dimensional waterfowl, bridges, and urban fauna. She bought some putty and stuck them to their apartment's bare walls. Tiny wondered why there were no pictures of him strung in between the other images.

*

Beth took Tiny to the Intrepid Sea, Air, & Space Museum, an aircraft carrier built in 1943 and parked on the Hudson River. They moved around the exhibit, his small hand in hers. Tiny was delighted by the Growler Submarine, with its top-secret missile command center, and the Space Shuttle Pavilion that housed the prototype NASA orbiter. At the end of their tour, he yanked her towards an open cockpit. He crawled inside and sat on the pilot's chair, grabbing the wheel, pretending to fly. "Pshew Pshew Pshew," he said, missile noises shooting from his mouth. There were two seats, and Beth took her place beside him. Their two seats were compact, and a window looked out across the Hudson River. She pushed her hand through his sandy head of hair and gently pulled him to her, remembering how strange she felt after her parents fell from the sky. She pressed into his arm with her hand, offering a rhythmic assurance. She was comforted by the small space, and wished it were a real flight that would take them far away. Tiny was now tall for ten years old. Beth's gestures across the last decade had added up to nurture this wiry boy into a curious being who needed more to feel. Between them, they had a constellation of issues. He was half her, and half Ahab, she remembered, looking across the wide river hoping to spot the fin of a whale.

BIOS

KUMMAM AL-MAADEED
Kummam Al-Maadeed is an author from Qatar, who believes in magic and the existence of fairy worlds. She started writing in 2007 when she was attending Qatar University to study Mass Communications. She now works at Qatar University as a Section Head of Media & Publications, as she dreams about her next novel. *The Lost Rose* is her debut best-selling novel.

SHIREEN ARORA
Shireen Arora is an Arizona resident. She likes to explore various art forms such as painting, calligraphy, writing poetry, playing the piano, and learning Indian classical dance.

RACHEL AYDT
Rachel Aydt is a part-time Assistant Professor of writing at the New School University. She also teaches a hybrid prose class at the Writing Institute of Sarah Lawrence College. She's published essays and short stories in *The White Review*, *HCE Review*, *Broad Street Journal*, *Post Road*, *Green Mountains Journal*, and many other publications, and has completed a memoir. She lives in New York City and is co-founder of the Crystal Radio Sessions series at the KGB Bar in Manhattan.

YUAN CHANGMING
Yuan Changming hails with Allen Yuan from poetrypacific.blogspot.ca. Credits include Pushcart nominations and appearances in *Best of the Best Canadian Poetry* (2008-17) & *BestNewPoemsOnline*, among others. Recently, Yuan served on the jury for Canada's 44th National Magazine Awards (poetry category).

MICKEY COLLINS
~~Mickey rights wrongs. Mickey wrongs rites.~~ Mickey writes words, sometimes wrong words but he tries to get it write.

BEN CROWLEY
Ben Crowley is from Pittsburgh, Pennsylvania. He is happy to get back to writing because he has already paid a kidney, three molars, a finger and a thumb to Deep Overstock and is weighing the value of his sensory organs. Ben used to sort books for the Amazon warehouse, in our beautiful

backcountry of western Pittsburgh.

JOHN DELANEY
In 2016, I moved out to Port Townsend, WA, after retiring as curator of historic maps at Princeton University Library. I've traveled widely, preferring remote, natural settings, and am addicted to kayaking and hiking. In 2017, I published *Waypoints* (Pleasure Boat Studio, Seattle), a collection of place poems. *Twenty Questions*, a chapbook, appeared in 2019 from Finishing Line Press.

DESIREE DUCHARME
Desiree Ducharme is a once and future Used Book Buyer, semi-feral dragon, who spends her days making space for dreams at Powell's City of Books as an Operations Manager. You can find more of her work at desireeducharme.com.

LYNETTE ESPOSITO
Lynette Esposito has been published in *Poetry Quarterly, Inwood Indiana, Walt Whitman Project, That Literary Review, North of Oxford*, and others. She was married to Attilio Esposito.

ROBERT EVERSMANN
Robert Eversmann works for Deep Overstock.

KATE FALVEY
Kate Falvey's work has been published in an eclectic array of journals and anthologies, including the Mysteries issue of *Deep Overstock*; in a full-length collection, *The Language of Little Girls* (David Robert Books); and in two chapbooks. She edits the *2 Bridges Review*, published through City Tech/ CUNY, where she teaches, and is an associate editor for the *Bellevue Literary Review*.

DORIS FERLEGER
Doris Ferleger is a winner of the New Letters Poetry Songs of Eretz Prize, Montgomery County Poet Laureate Prize, Robert Fraser Poetry Prize, and the AROHO Creative Non-Fiction Prize, among others. In 2020 she was nominated for the Pushcart Prize by *Delmarva Review*. She is the author of three full volumes of poetry: *Big Silences in a Year of Rain* (finalist for the Alice James Books/Beatrice Hawley Award), *As the Moon Has Breath*, and *Leavened*, as well as a chapbook entitled *When You Become Snow*. Her work has been published in numerous journals including *The Cape Rock, Cider Press Review, Cimarron Review, DASH Literary Journal, Delmarva Review, El Portal, Euphony, Evening Street Review, Glint*

Literary Journal, Good Works Review, L.A. Review, Meadow, Off the Coast, Packingtown Review, Poet Lore, Rougarou, The Virginia Normal, Whimperbang, Whistling Shade, and *South Carolina Review.* She holds an MFA in Poetry and a PhD in Psychology and maintains a mindfulness-based therapy practice in Wyncote, PA.

JO GRIFFIN

Jo Griffin is an aspiring author and podcaster from the Pacific Northwest who loves D&D, Mothman, and Hawaiian shirts. She writes to reconnect new adults with reading for pleasure, and spends way too much money at bookstores.

BOGDAN GROZA

I was born in Romania and am currently living in Italy. I finished a Master's Degree programme in European, American and Postcolonial Language and Literature at the faculty of Padua. I have been writing since I was about eighteen and several short stories and poems found their way in minor Italian anthologies. I recently managed to publish my first book, *Athena,* with a small publishing company.

LEORA JOY JONES

Leora Joy Jones is a poet, photographer, writer, and arts practitioner. She is interested in the perverted intersections between art, the practise of everyday life, and popular culture. Recently, her art criticism has been trained on ecological art practises and their potential to shift the ways in which people perceive their relationship with the environment. Born in the USA, and raised in South Africa, she now lives and works in Taiwan. Leora holds a degree in Fine Art from the university currently known as Rhodes, and is earning an MA in Critical and Curatorial Studies of Contemporary Art (CCSCA) in Taipei. A founder of the Taipei Poetry Collective, Leora hosts readings and biweekly poetry workshops. She is assistant editor at southerly journal, and her writing can be found in *Yishu Journal of Contemporary Chinese Art, ArtAsiaPacific, Design Anthology,* the *Newslens International* and *Southerly Journal.* You can see more of her photography at leorajoy.com and on instagram.com/loveleorajoy.

RYAN SHANE LOPEZ

Ryan Shane Lopez is an English teacher with an MFA in fiction from Texas State University. His writing has appeared in numerous magazines, including *Hypnopomp, Deep Overstock, Porter House Review, Lunate, Fudoki, Patheos, Bodega,* and *The Bookends Review.* He lives in Texas with his wife, Hannah, and their two daughters.

WALTER MOON

walter moon has been lost in books since birth and bookselling in one way
or another for almost 20 years. living in portland with his partner, Nat, and
their companion, Mishka, he strives to find the key to immortality but has
trouble locating the key to his house.

TIMOTHY ARLISS OBRIEN

Timothy Arliss OBrien is an interdisciplinary artist in music composition,
writing, and visual arts. His goal is to connect people to accessible new
music that showcases virtuosic abilities without losing touch of authentic
emotions. He has premiered music with The Astoria Music Festival,
Cascadia Composers, Sound of Late's 48 hour Composition Competition
and ENAensemble's Serial Opera Project. He also wants to produce writing
that connects the reader to themselves in a way that promotes wonder and
self realization. He has published several novels (Dear God I'm a Faggot,
They), several cartomancy decks for divination (The Gazing Ball Tarot, The
Graffiti Oracle, and The Ink Sketch Lenormand), and has written for Look
Up Records (Seattle), Our Bible App, and Deep Overstock: The Bookseller's
Journal. He has also combined his passion for poetry with his love of
publishing and curates the podcast The Poet Heroic and he also hosts the
new music podcast Composers Breathing. He also showcases his psychedelic
makeup skills as the phenomenal drag queen Tabitha Acidz.
Check out more of his writing, and his full discography at his website: www.
timothyarlissobrien.com

FARNIFF P.

Farnilf P. is a member of a pseudonymous arts collective dedicated to
world domination. An ephemeral art book of this work is forthcoming
from PiNPRESS.online, and the author is in negotiations with Evil Portent
Publishing for a children's picture book edition.

DAVID JAMES PUSSANT

I am the author of the novel *Lake Life* (Simon & Schuster, 2020), a *New
York Times* Editors' Choice selection, *Publishers Weekly* Summer Read, and
a *Millions* Most Anticipated Book of 2020. My story collection *The Heaven
of Animals* was a winner of the GLCA New Writers Award and a Florida
Book Award, a finalist for the L.A. Times Book Prize, and was longlisted for
the PEN/Robert W. Bingham Prize. My stories and essays have appeared
in *The Atlantic Monthly*, *The Chicago Tribune*, *The New York Times*, *One
Story*, *Ploughshares*, *The Southern Review*, and in numerous textbooks
and anthologies including *New Stories from the South*, *Best New American
Voices*, and *Best American Experimental Writing*. My books are currently
in print in six languages. I teach in the MFA Program in Creative Writing

at the University of Central Florida and live in Orlando with my wife and daughters.

Vicky Ruan
Vicky Ruan lives in Taiwan. She has worked for a publishing company for two years as an editor in charge of English and Japanese learning books. Vicky is interested in history, games, movies, and fantasy. Vicky treats her work with responsibility and passion, believing that books are a necessary part of our lives.

Viviann Ruiz
When Viviann Ruiz isn't working as a library assistant they can be found drawing either in their local park or at home. Taking artistic inspiration from movies and video games. Most of their art can be found at glynloryl@ tumblr.com.

Michael Santiago
Michael Santiago is a serial expat, avid traveler, and writer of all kinds. Originally from New York City, and later relocating to Rome in 2016 and Nanjing in 2018. He enjoys the finer things in life like walks on the beach, existential conversations and swapping murder mystery ideas. Keen on exploring themes of humanity within a fictitious context and aspiring author.

Hibah Shabkhez
Hibah Shabkhez is a writer of the half-yo literary tradition, an erratic language-learning enthusiast, and a happily eccentric blogger from Lahore, Pakistan. Her work has previously appeared in *Zin Daily*, *Litbreak*, *Broadkill*, *Rising Phoenix*, *Big City Lit*, *Constellate*, *Harpy Hybrid*, and a number of other literary magazines. Studying life, languages, and literature from a comparative perspective across linguistic and cultural boundaries holds a particular fascination for her. Linktree: https://linktr.ee/HibahShabkhez

Jihye Shin
Jihye Shin is a 1.5-generation Korean-American bookseller in Florida. Her work focuses on the poetics of the analog-digital, liminial and futurist differences. She is also the creator of a text-based interactive game called Goodnight, Starlight. Her professional website is www.jihyeshin.ink.

K. B. Thomas
K. B. Thomas has been a book lover and bookseller since dinosaurs roamed the earth. She works, writes, and walks her dog in Portland, OR. Find more fiction at: kbthomas.net

Eric Thralby

Captain by trade, Cpt. Eric Thralby works wood in his long off-days. He time-to-time pilots the Bremerton Ferry (Bremerton—Vashon; Vahon—Bremerton), while other times sells books on amazon.com, SellerID: plainpages. He'll sell any books the people love, strolling down to library and yard sales, but he loves especially books of Romantic fiction, not of risqué gargoyles, not harlequin romance, but knights, errant or of the Table. Eric has not published before, but has read in local readings at the Gig Harbor Candy Company and the Lavender Inne, also in Gig Harbor.

Jonathan van Belle

Jonathan van Belle is the author of *Zenithism* (2021) from Deep Overstock Publishing, Editor-in-Chief at Z-Sky (zsky.org), a Content Creator at Outlier.org, and a fan of mallsoft music. You can find his cardboard cutout at www.jonathanvanbelle.com.

Z.B. Wagman

Z.B. Wagman is an editor for the Deep Overstock Literary Journal and a co-host of the Deep Overstock Fiction podcast. When not writing or editing he can be found behind the desk at the Beaverton City Library, where he finds much inspiration.

Nicholas Yandell

Nicholas Yandell is a composer, who sometimes creates with words instead of sound. In those cases, he usually ends up with fiction and occasionally poetry. He also paints and draws, and often all these activities become combined, because they're really not all that different from each other, and it's all just art right?
When not working on creative projects, Nick works as a bookseller at Powell's Books in Portland, Oregon, where he enjoys being surrounded by a wealth of knowledge, as well as working and interacting with creatively stimulating people. He has a website where he displays his creations; it's nicholasyandell.com. Check it out!